W9-CPF-135

OTHER YEARLING BOOKS YOU WILL ENJOY:

The Velvet Room

WRITTEN BY
ZILPHA KEATLEY SNYDER

ILLUSTRATED BY ALTON RAIBLE

A YEARLING BOOK

Published by
Dell Publishing
a division of
The Bantam Doubleday Dell Publishing Group, Inc.
666 Fifth Avenue
New York, New York 10103

ISBN: 0-440-40042-2

Reprinted by arrangement with Macmillan Publishing Company on behalf of Atheneum Publishers

Printed in the United States of America

April 1988

10 9 8 7 6 5 4 3 2

CW

To Larry

Contents

The Velvet Room

Breakdown

WHEN THE TIRE went flat for the third time that day, it went with a bang. The car swerved sharply to the left and then to the right and came to a sudden stop. Robin's chin hit something, perhaps her own knee, and she bit her tongue. Shirley was screaming, and for a minute Robin's eyes were blinded with tears. But she blinked them away and stuck her head out of the window. Cary was pushing and tromping, trying to get his head out of the window in front of Robin's.

Robin gasped when she saw what the car had hit. For the first time she was thankful that the poor old Model T couldn't go very fast any more. What if they'd hit all those stones at fifty miles an hour?

The car doors spilled open, and they all poured out: Dad from the driver's seat, and Cary and Theda and Rudy from the back. Mama was slower because Shirley was still hanging around her neck and yelling as if she were being killed.

3

But Robin just sat. She tucked her legs up on the seat and rubbed her bare toes where Cary had just about smashed them as he climbed out over her.

Dad was standing in front of the car, shaking his head slowly from side to side. "Well, that does it," he said. "That just about does it." He didn't look angry or even worried, any more—just tired.

But Cary looked positively delighted, "Lookit the wheel, Dad. Gee! Lookit the fender!" He jerked at Dad's sleeve and jumped up and down as if he were looking at a clown in a circus. It seemed to Robin that even an eight-year-old ought to know better.

Mama finally managed to unfasten Shirley from around her neck long enough to climb out of the front seat; but when Shirley saw how the fender and wheel were smashed flat against the pillar of stones, she began to scream all over again. She buried her face in Mama's skirt and wailed.

"There, there, Shirley honey," Mama said. "Don't cry. You know it's bad for you to cry so hard."

Robin smiled with tight lips. It wasn't that Shirley was old enough to realize just how bad a fix they were in; it was only that she never missed an opportunity to howl no matter what happened. And even though it was bad for her asthma, no one ever made her shut up.

"There, there, Shirley," Mama was still saying. "There's no need to take on so. Rudy can fix it. Just look, Shirley honey. Rudy's getting ready to fix it right now."

Shirley took her face out of Mama's skirt for a second to glance at Rudy. It didn't take her long to decide that Rudy wasn't doing anything that would make watching more fun than yelling, so she went right back to yelling.

Robin sighed. Rudy didn't seem to be doing anything except squatting beside the squashed wheel, touching it lightly with his fingers as if he were trying to take its pulse. Of course, if anybody could fix it Rudy could, even though he was only fifteen. Rudy might not be very good at some things, but, as Dad said, a sick machine seemed to be able to tell Rudy where it hurt.

But this might be too much even for Rudy. What could a boy of fifteen, with only a few tools, do for a wheel that looked like that? No, it was ruined. The car was ruined, and it was over a hundred miles to where Dad was supposed to get a job.

Robin pulled her legs up against her chest and wrapped her faded print skirt and thin brown arms tightly around them. She rested her chin on her knees and rocked herself to and fro.

She was beginning to have a strange feeling. It wasn't the first time she had felt this way. Everything seemed to be moving backward away from her, getting smaller and smaller, less and less real. It was as if she were watching everything from a long way off. There beyond the cracked windshield was her family, gathered noisily around the broken wheel, and closer yet was the back of the front seat, with the patches of gunny sacking sewn on over the torn upholstery. Closest of all were her own bare toes, a little bit dirty, sticking out from under the cotton skirt. But all of it —even the dirty toes—seemed quite unreal.

Robin opened the car door and jumped out. She looked quickly around. Directly in front of her was a high gate of twisted-looking black metal. The gate hung from two huge stone pillars. It was against one of these pillars that the old car had met its fate. From the tops of the tall columns of stone more black metal, in an elaborate pattern of leaves and flowers, formed an arch above the gate. In the midst of this arch the metal had been shaped into fancy letters forming the words Las Palmeras. Through the bars of the gate Robin could see a curving road, weed-grown and potholed, but lined on both sides by a wonderful procession of gigantic palm trees.

The gate was too high to climb over, but beyond the pillars the stone fence was lower. Robin easily found places to fit her bare toes. Just as she was on her stomach on top of the wall, ready to drop down on the other side, Mama saw her.

"Robin," she called. "What are you doing up there?" She started toward the wall, but because Shirley was still crying into her skirt she couldn't move very quickly.

"I'm just climbing over, Mama, to look around."

"If that's somebody's yard over there, you're going to be trespassing," Mama said in her sternest voice.

"Oh, it's not, Mama." Robin was getting breathless from hanging over the stone wall on her stomach. "It's just an orchard and an old deserted road." Without waiting for an answer, she shoved off and dropped to the ground.

Mama's voice came over the wall. "Don't you go wandering off again, Robin. You stay within shouting distance. You hear?"

"Yes, Mama," Robin shouted back as she started off through the knee-deep weeds of the old road.

The House of the Palms

ALTHOUGH the summer fog of coastal California had been thick all morning as they drove, the skies were now clear. Slanting rays of afternoon sun threw the long shadows of the palms far to the east. Across the old road lay only the narrow shadows of the trunks, making a striped pattern of sun and shade. Beyond the palms, on each side of the road, were rows and rows of orange trees, their waxy leaves like green glass in the sunshine and almost black in the shade.

As Robin walked slowly up the center of the road, a sudden contentment replaced the feeling that had sent her scrambling over the wall a few minutes before. It was quiet here, away from the noise of the highway and all the rush and roar of people. The air smelled of sun-warmed earth and orange blossoms. But it was the palms, more than anything else, that brought a strange feeling of peace.

They were very old trees. Their heads, shaggy with untrimmed fronds, reached far into the air, and their huge trunks were scarred with age. Bordering the abandoned

7

road like the ancient pillars of some ruined temple, they marked the way far into the distance. Robin thought they were probably the oldest trees she had ever seen.

A little farther on, the road curved over a gentle rise. From the top Robin could see a thick grove of trees at the base of the hills. She looked back uneasily. It was a lot more than shouting distance back to the highway. She really ought to go back. But she knew that nothing could make her return until she had seen what was hidden behind that grove of trees.

As she approached, she could see that these trees, too, were very old and very large. They were mostly oak and peppers, with here and there some others she didn't recognize. The road, even more weed-choked, curved now through almost twilight shade. It curved some more and suddenly came to—a house.

It was about the largest house that Robin had ever seen. It was built of pale gray stone, and at one end it had a high round tower. A long portico supported by stone arches ran all around the front and one side.

It was a wonderful house, almost like a castle—but after a moment Robin realized that something was terribly wrong. On the bottom floor there were no windows. Every place a window should have been there were only rough planks. The house looked wounded; like a beautiful face with bandages for eyes.

Robin was standing at the edge of a large clearing that once must have been a lawn. In the center of the clearing was a stone-lined pool in which three bronze sea horses stood on a pedestal. The dry pool was littered with dead leaves, and the round mouths of the sea horses were full of dust.

How different it all must have looked when the windows sparkled with sunlight, when the fountain splashed, and the lawn was green; when the porches weren't cluttered with dirt and branches, and the curving road that swept before the door was white with fresh gravel.

It made Robin angry. How could the people it belonged to treat it that way? To let it sit there dead and lonely with its windows blinded! If it were hers, she would never have done that to it. If it were her house, she would look out of every window every day, and just be happy to be there. Just be happy to live in a house that seemed to have grown up out of the hills behind it.

"Robin!" Even though Theda was still a long way off, her voice was plainly exasperated. She must have been calling for a long time.

"Coming!" Robin shouted, and with a quick backward look at the old house, she started toward the highway. She ran fast, hoping to stop Theda before she reached the grove of trees that hid the house. She didn't know why it was so important to keep Theda from seeing the house, but it was.

She needn't have worried. Theda, plainly, hadn't come any farther after she had heard Robin's answering call. Breathless from running, Robin topped the rise in the road and saw her sitting on an irrigation weir at the edge of the orchard. She had one shoe off and was rubbing her foot.

"Where have you been?" she demanded crossly, slipping her shoe back on. "Didn't you hear Mama tell you not to wander off?"

"I didn't wander off," Robin gasped. "I was just walking, and I didn't notice how far I had gone."

"Well, we just ought to go off and leave you some time," Theda grumbled. "Serve you right. Always wandering around with your head in the clouds."

Robin glanced quickly at Theda. It wasn't like her to be so cross. You couldn't count on Theda for a lot of important things, but you could usually count on her to be cheerful—even when there wasn't a thing in the world to be cheerful about. They walked on silently for a while before it occurred to Robin that Theda's grouchiness was probably because of sore feet.

Just before they left the camp in Salinas, a woman had given Theda a pair of high-heeled pumps. Mama said that fourteen was too young for high heels, but Theda had finally talked her into changing her mind. Theda had been wearing the pumps for the last two days; but since they'd been in the car almost constantly, she still hadn't had much walking practice. Now, as she made her way carefully over the rough surface of the old road, her ankles wobbled and her freckled face looked pained.

"Why don't you take them off till we get back near the highway?" Robin suggested. "Nobody's going to see you out here in the orchard, anyway."

Theda's lips tightened, and she shook her head. She could be surprisingly determined sometimes, particularly if it had anything to do with clothes. If there was anything that really mattered to Theda, besides boys of course, it was what she was or wasn't going to wear.

The iron gates were in sight now; and for the first time since she had fallen under the spell of the ancient palms, Robin thought about the mess they were in. "What are they going to do?" she asked. "About the car, I mean."

Theda shrugged. "Rudy got the wheel clear off, and he and Dad went off to look for a service station. Rudy said they'd have to buy a whole new wheel, but Dad thought they might get it straightened out."

Robin's brow furrowed. Rudy was probably right—he

usually was when it came to machinery—and Robin knew that Dad had only about twelve dollars left to last them until they got to San Bernardino. He'd said so last night when Mama wanted to take the kids to the movies to see the new Shirley Temple picture. Could you get a whole new wheel and tire for twelve dollars? And even if you could, what about food and gas all the rest of the way there?

"I wonder how much a wheel costs?" she asked Theda. "Dad doesn't have much money left. I heard him say so."

"Who cares!" You could tell that Theda's sophisticated shrug was copied from someone in the movies, but Robin couldn't think just who. "Don't worry about it. We'll get there somehow. We always do. There's always the police, you know. They'll probably see that we get as far as the next county, anyway. Remember how helpful they were that time we broke down right in the middle of Pasadena?"

Robin clenched her teeth. How could Theda joke about that time in Pasadena! It made a pain in Robin's stomach just to think about it. Everyone staring, and those awful policemen laughing about all the stuff tied on top of the car and making jokes about "Okies." Robin had tried to tell one of them how the Williamses weren't "Okies," or "Arkies," either; but the policeman had just grinned and said, "Well, you couldn't tell by looking, kid."

Robin broke into a run and scrambled over the stone wall, leaving Theda to get over as best she could in her silly high heels. Mama and Shirley were sitting in the front seat, and Mama was reading the funny paper to Shirley. Robin knew for a fact that it was at least the tenth time that someone had read that same ragged funny paper to her. Cary was up on top of the load on the roof of the Model T. He was sitting astraddle the rolled up mattress, pretending to be riding a horse. There was no sign of Dad or Rudy.

End of a Three-Year Journey

JUST AS Robin was climbing into the back seat over the roll of bedding on the running board, a big new truck slowed up and made a U turn in the highway right in front of them. To everyone's surprise, there in the back of the truck were Dad and Rudy. The truck stopped, they jumped down, and two strange men got out of the cab. Or rather one strange man and a boy: a thick, awkward-looking boy, as big as a man, but with a not-quite-finished look about him.

Theda had just made it over the wall, and was teetering toward the car, smoothing her hair and tucking in her blouse and trying to pretend she hadn't noticed the strange boy. Mama, followed by Shirley, got out of the car and pretty soon everyone was standing around in front of the car again. That is, everyone except Cary, who stayed on the roof, and Robin, who just sat in the corner of the back seat.

"Helen," Dad said, "this is Mr. Criley and his boy, Fred. Mr. Criley, this is my wife, Mrs. Williams, and my family. You met my eldest, Rudy here, and then there's

Theda, and Robin—where is Robin?" Mama nodded toward the car. "Oh, there she is over in the car. Robin's twelve now. And Cary—up there on the load. He's eight and the baby, here, is four." Dad patted Shirley on the head; she promptly stuck her thumb in her mouth and ducked behind Mama.

Robin watched Mr. Criley's eyes move slowly and coolly over each of them. His head nodded briefly in acknowledgment of the introductions. For a long minute he looked at the ancient Model T with its top-heavy load of household possessions. As Robin looked at Mr. Criley, in a funny sort of way she also saw exactly what he was seeing. She could see every detail: every dent and paintless patch of rusted metal, every cracked or broken window. She could see exactly how the boxes and bags and rolls looked that were piled and tied on every inch of the roof and even on the running boards. For three years the Model T had been the only unchanging part of her life; and though she realized how important the car was to them, it seemed as if every one of those more-than-a-thousand days had made her hate the old car a little more.

Mr. Criley's inspection finally appeared to be over because he turned to Dad abruptly and said, "The car will have to stay here for now. Too late to fool with it today. But you'd better bring everything else along if you don't want it to get stolen." His lips curved upward in what was supposed to be a smile, but seemed like something very different. "Don't think you need to worry about anybody stealing that car." He turned back to the truck. As he climbed into the cab, he shouted, "Better put all them younguns to work on that load. I got to get back to the ranch."

Dad didn't even give Theda and Mama a chance to ask

any questions. His voice had a new sound, firmer and more lively, as he said, "O.K. everybody. Let's see how fast we can get all our stuff into the back of the truck. Step lively now. Theda, you take the bedding. Rudy, you get those boxes of kitchen things. Robin! Get out of that car and lend a hand here. Mama, I'll boost you and Shirley up, and you can push the things back in the truck bed as we hand them up."

In a minute there were Williamses running in every direction. The boy named Fred had not gotten back into the truck with his father. At first Robin wondered if he was thinking of helping them. But he only stood there, leaning against the side of the truck and watching, as he tossed a coin up and down with one hand. He was big and strong looking, and maybe as old as eighteen even; but his face was pink and lumpy, like a big homely baby. Something about the expression on his face made Robin's eyes fill with angry tears. When the car was almost empty, he slowly and deliberately stood himself up straight and strolled over to it. Robin was inside collecting the last few things, Cary's sweater and Shirley's old rag doll. The boy named Fred leaned on his hands on the window sill and with lifted eyebrows carefully surveyed the interior of the Model T. Kneeling on the back seat, Robin stared back at him angrily, but he didn't even seem to see her.

He was allowing his lips to curve into a slow, scornful smile when suddenly there was a loud whack! The scornful expression dissolved instantly into one of pained surprise. There was nothing slow or deliberate about the way he pulled his head out of the car and stood up. Robin scrambled over to the window in time to see him glaring down at Cary and rubbing the seat of his trousers.

Cary had Dad's shovel over his shoulder. The expres-

sion on his round, freckled face was a caricature of shocked
innocence, but Robin was only too familiar with the wicked
twinkle in his blue eyes.

"Gee!" Cary said, "I'm sorry. I just had this old shovel,
and when I turned around I didn't see where the end of it
was going. See, I just turned around quick like this and . . ."
Cary demonstrated, whirling around quickly, so that this
time the shovel whistled by the bigger boy's stomach.

"Hey! Watch it!" the boy yelled, jumping backward
so quickly that he almost lost his balance and fell. He re-
gained his balance but not his dignity and, still holding the
injured area, retreated to the truck.

Robin and Cary looked at each other. That gleam in
Cary's eye usually made Robin want to wring his neck. She
regarded him soberly for a long thoughtful moment. Then
very slowly they smiled at each other.

When, at last, all of the Williamses and their worldly
possessions were piled into the truck, Mr. Criley started off
down the highway with a screech of gears that scared
Shirley into another crying spell. Over Shirley's yelling and
the roar of the truck's motor, Dad explained what had
happened and why they were all bouncing around in the
back of the truck.

"I have a job!" he said, and Robin noticed again the
difference in his voice. It was as if for the first time in
months he liked the sound of what he was saying. "At least
till the end of apricot season and maybe even afterwards.
Strangest thing. Rudy and I stopped in at a big ranch just
a half mile or so up the road to ask where we could find
a service station. There was a sign out front that said Las
Palmeras, same as back there on the gatepost we ran into.
We just got inside the gate when a man on a horse rode
over and asked us what we wanted. I told him about the

fix we were in, and he started asking a lot of questions about my experience with mules and citrus and if the family was all healthy . . ."

"Was it that Mr. Criley, on the horse?" Mama interrupted.

"Oh, no," Dad said. "Mr. Criley's just a foreman. The fellow on the horse was Mr. McCurdy himself. Owns I don't know how many hundred acres around here. Seems to be a real nice fellow, too. So anyway, he said that one of his permanent hands quit on him just this morning. He said I can work until the end of apricot season at least, and maybe longer if I fill the bill."

As Dad was talking, a question trembled on Robin's tongue until she felt she would strangle if she didn't ask it. "Dad!" she nearly shouted, but when Dad turned to her in surprise she could hardly ask for fear the answer would be the wrong one. "Dad, does a house come with the job? I mean, if it's a permanent job maybe a real house of our own comes with it."

Dad smiled and put his arm across her shoulders. "Mr. McCurdy said he provides houses for all his permanent hands. Of course, I haven't seen it yet, but there is a house, Big Enough, and we'll be seeing it in just a few minutes."

Robin looked up quickly at Dad's smiling face. He used to call her Big Enough a lot, but that had been a long time ago; it seemed like years and years—so long ago that all she had had to worry about was being too small.

Despair

THE NEXT MORNING Robin sat on the front steps of her new home with her chin in her hands. The very thing that they had all been praying for had happened—Dad had found a permanent job. But at that moment, there on the stairs, on that June morning in 1937, she was thinking that the word for how she was feeling was—despair.

Despair was like climbing up a mountain trying to escape from a terrible desert. You struggle on for ages and ages, because you keep thinking that someday you'll have to reach the top. And then at last you come to the summit and you look over—and before you is another thousand miles of desert. And this time it is worse, so much worse, because now you know there's no way to escape.

She realized that she had been foolish. She had hoped for so long that Dad would get a steady job that she had gotten into the habit of thinking that when he did everything would be perfect. It was three years since the depression and the mortgages had made Dad lose his place in

Fresno. They had been three years of living in tents and shacks and even in the old Model T; so a steady job for Dad had started to mean more than anything else, a house to live in: a real house with a front porch, shiny floors, and things around that were there just to be beautiful, like pictures and curtains.

Robin leaned forward and hid her face on her knees. Her eyes felt hot, but she was not going to cry. "What's the matter with you, anyway," she told herself. "You should have known better."

But she hadn't known better. At least she hadn't last night when Dad had said that a house came with the job on Mr. McCurdy's ranch. How happy she'd been for a few minutes.

Then the truck had turned off the highway and crunched along a graveled road beside a hedge. Over the hedge Robin had caught sight of a very large house. Trees and shrubs had partly blocked the view, but Robin had gotten an impression of huge gleaming white surfaces, rounded corners, and large expanses of sparkling glass.

Behind the big modern house there was another broad expanse of tree-studded lawn, and beyond that, a long low wooden building that gleamed immaculately white, even in the twilight. From a double door in the building a horse's sleek black head had emerged; he was still chewing a mouthful of hay. Beyond the stables the truck had passed through a large dust-whitened yard, surrounded by a confusion of buildings—barnlike structures of various sizes and open sheds full of farm machinery.

Just beyond the barns Robin had seen something that had made her heart stumble for a moment. Set apart by a white picket fence, a neat little house sat securely on a patch of green lawn. But the truck hadn't stopped, and as they passed she had noticed that clothes were blowing on a line behind the house. She had known then that it wasn't the one, but perhaps she had thought, theirs would be like it. She knew now that the white house was where the Crileys lived; and they lived there because Mr. Criley was a foreman. But she hadn't known that last night.

Just beyond the Criley's house the road changed from gravel to badly rutted dirt, and Robin had been forced to hang on tightly to the slats of the truck bed. Ahead she had seen a windbreak—a thickly planted row of towering eucalyptus trees. The rutted road passed through a narrow opening in the row of trees and came to a sudden stop. And there in the narrow alley between the eucalyptus windbreak and the first row of the orange orchard was Las Palmeras

Village—the Williamses' new home. It had been right then that Robin had found out about despair.

She was still pressing her forehead hard against her knees and squeezing her eyes shut when the noise of an approaching car brought a welcome interruption. She lifted her head to see a Packard coupé shudder over the deep ruts of the road and come to a stop a few feet from the steps on which she was sitting. A small man bustled out of the car carrying a leather bag.

"You one of the Williamses?" he asked.

Robin frowned. "I'm Robin," she said. She thought of saying "I'm not one of anything," but she didn't.

But the little man didn't wait for an answer anyway. He trotted on up the stairs to where Mama opened the door just as he was about to knock on it. Mama looked startled.

"Mrs. Williams?" he said. "I'm Doctor Woods. Mr. McCurdy sent me around to see you folks."

Theda stopped brushing her hair, and Rudy got up off the floor where he had been trying to plug up a hole in the bottom of the wood stove. His face and hands were smeared with soot. Cary was under the table. Mama tried to make some room for the doctor's bag, and some tin plates got shoved off the table onto the floor. Mama and the doctor both reached for them and almost bumped heads.

"Excuse me," Mama said, "excuse me. I'm sorry to have you see us in such a mess, Doctor." Her voice sounded too high, the way it did when she was embarrassed, and she kept trying to smooth down Shirley's wispy, uncombed hair with her hands. "We just got in last night and . . ."

"Of course, of course," the doctor boomed. "Now if you children will just line up here . . ."

"I don't understand why Mr. McCurdy sent . . ."

Mama interrupted herself, "that is, I mean nobody's been sick, except of course Shirley here had just a touch of asthma last night, but . . ."

"Of course, of course," Doctor Woods said again, digging into his bag. "Just a precaution. Mr. McCurdy likes to be sure the folks who live here in the Village are in good health—being so close to the big house and all." He deftly scooped Shirley out from behind Mama and pried her mouth open. "Say ah! That's a girl."

He poked and peered his way down the line, teasing Theda and joking with Cary. Robin was last. "Well, well. Here's the little bitty girl with the big eyes," he said. "Let's take a look at you. Don't look much like your brothers and sisters, do you? Now just open your mouth. That's the way. You the last one or are there five or six more around somewhere?" Robin was glad the depressor was holding her tongue down so she didn't have to answer.

But Theda did. "There's Dad," she said. "He's working."

"Already saw your dad. Mr. Criley told me where to find him, so I just stopped off at the mule barn on my way down here." He began putting things back in the bag. "Well, you folks have a clean bill of health for the time being, Mrs. Williams. But you ought to try to get a little meat on those kids' bones. Particularly that little one. Lots of milk would help."

As soon as the doctor's car bounced away through the gap in the eucalyptus trees, Robin drifted out the door and down the steps. She went slowly because if she hurried someone might guess she was doing what the family called "wandering off" and try to stop her. And she just had to get away.

Bridget

LAS PALMERAS VILLAGE was a row of twelve two-room
cabins. At one time they had been covered with a coat of
yellow paint, but that had obviously been long ago. They
sat up off the ground on foundations of narrow poles, so
that to Robin they looked like boxcars with wooden legs
instead of wheels. They had a movable, unattached look.
It wasn't a bit hard to imagine the whole string of them
stumping off stiffly through the orchard. But of course,
they didn't. Instead they just crouched there on their
wooden legs, each one only a few feet from its nearest
neighbors. A few pale weeds had found an unhealthy refuge
under the houses, but everywhere else the soil of the village
had been scoured smooth by many feet. Its barren, dusty
surface was varied only by occasional piles of trash, broken
boxes, and rusty tin cans. Halfway down the row of cabins,
Robin passed the rickety wooden building that held the
toilets, the showers, and the laundry tubs for the whole
village.

A Mexican girl of about Robin's age was coming out of the laundry room carrying a bucket of wet clothing. She had big dark eyes and long black braids. She smiled shyly and said, "Allo."

Robin smiled back, but she didn't stop. Just now she was in a hurry. Before she reached the end of the row of cabins, she began to run. When she came to the orchard, she went on running, but more slowly because the furrowed ground was rough and uneven. Every once in a while she stopped and looked around. By finding the hills over the tops of the orange trees, she could judge her direction. She was sure that if she kept on going south and then turned toward the hills, she would sooner or later come to the stone house.

It wasn't as far as she thought it would be. Before she was even completely out of breath from running, she saw ahead of her the tops of the tall shade trees that surrounded the house. She cut toward the hills past two more aisles of orange trees, turned south again, and in just a moment she had come to a stone wall. Climbing over it, she dodged around some tangled shrubbery, and there it was.

Before her the stone walls of the house rose high with timeless strength. Once you got used to the idea, it didn't seem to matter very much that the downstairs windows were boarded up and the lawn was a ruined tangle. It wasn't frightening like other deserted houses. Robin had seen many frightening ones in the last three years—ruined rinds of houses, their doors gaping and windows staring blankly. But this house only waited, as peaceful as the hills that lay behind it.

After a while Robin wanted to see more and began to walk slowly around the house. It was three stories high, counting what seemed to be some attic rooms with gable windows and a round room in the top part of the tower. Apparently there were three round tower rooms, one on each floor. It was hard to guess just how many rooms there were, but Robin thought there must be at least twenty—maybe even more.

Behind the main part of the house Robin came upon a wing that looked very different. It was lower and was not made of stone. In places where the rough plaster had fallen away, she could see the surface of adobe bricks. She had seen bricks like that before. Once when they were going through Ventura, they had stopped for groceries on the main street right near the old Spanish mission. Robin had been peeking in the door when a priest came along and said it was all right to go in. She had been all alone in the huge old church. The thick adobe wall shut out the noises of the town, but the deep hush had seemed alive with ancient echoes.

The adobe wing of the house had a two-story veranda with wooden pillars and wrought-iron railings. The veranda faced a patio whose brick paving was scarcely visible through the dirt and debris. In the center of the patio was what seemed to be a boarded-up well, and near it was a second fountain. But this fountain was crumbling with age, and the stone figure in the center was chipped and broken until it was impossible to tell what it had once represented.

From the brick patio another stone building was just visible among the trees. It was long and low, and as Robin walked toward it she decided it must once have been a stable or a garage. But before she had come close enough to be sure, she saw something that made her change her direction. The first rolling dips of the foothills began just a few yards ahead, and from the shelter of a tree-covered mound there rose a thin white twist of smoke.

Curiosity and apprehension seesawed in Robin's mind as she rounded the wooded rise and saw before her a scene from a storybook.

A tiny stone house with a rough, shake roof sat up to its diamond-paned windows in hollyhocks and roses, looking like something from another time and place. A neat but faded picket fence enclosed the house and garden. Under the hollyhocks a half dozen black and white speckled chickens scratched and pecked.

Robin was just thinking that you could almost believe that three bears or perhaps seven dwarfs were going to appear in the doorway, when quite suddenly the door opened and a woman came out. It happened so quickly there was no time to hide. The woman moved toward Robin slowly, leaning on a cane. When she reached the gate, she unlatched it and held it open, smiling and nodding her head.

It was all so strange and unexpected that Robin was frightened. It was no use telling herself that a tiny, crippled lady was harmless. For one ridiculous moment Hansel and Gretel flitted through her mind. But she didn't run.

She didn't run because of the way she sometimes had of switching places with people in her mind. For just a split second, *she* was standing there behind the gate, holding it open with an unsteady hand and watching the fear in someone's eyes. So, although she wasn't at all comfortable about it, she walked up to the gate and said, "Hello."

"Hello, my dear," the woman said. From up close she didn't look old. She was small and a little bent and her hair was white, but her face was not deeply lined. Her cheeks were pink, and her small chin came to a youthful point. "It's so nice of you to come calling. Have you just been over at Palmeras House?"

"I guess so," Robin said. "I've been to that big stone house over there. Do you think anyone minds? I was only looking at it."

"I don't think anyone would mind in that case," the woman said. She turned slowly and led the way around the house on a narrow path among the flowers. "Have you been there before?"

"Just once," Robin said, "but I want to go back some more if no one cares. I like it there. Do you know who owns it?"

The woman stopped and turned to Robin smiling. "Why, the McCurdys own it, child. All the land for a mile or so on every side of us belongs to the McCurdys. "I'm surprised you don't know that. Aren't you from the Village?"

For just a minute Robin wondered how the woman knew. Then she glanced down at her bare feet and too-small faded dress. She supposed she looked like a Village girl. She moved her arm quickly to cover the rip at the waist of her dress.

"Yes, I live at the Village," she said. "But we just moved in yesterday. I don't know much about it."

The woman nodded. When they reached the back of the little stone house, she said, "I thought you might like to meet the rest of my family. But perhaps I should introduce myself first. I'm called Bridget. And what is your name?"

"I'm Robin, Robin Williams. Don't you . . . I mean should I call you just Bridget?"

"That will be fine. I don't bother with the rest of my name much any more."

The back door of the stone cottage opened into a small yard of hard-packed earth, which was surrounded by gardens on both sides. To the rear were two small sheds, which opened into fenced animal yards. The earthen floor of the little backyard had been swept clean, and a weathered rocking chair sat in the shade of an apricot tree near the house. On a bench near the back door Robin noticed a big ball of black and gray fur. The lady named Bridget patted the ball of fur, and it rolled apart and sat up—two separate animals. One was a large gray cat, but the other was—Robin gasped with surprise.

"A raccoon!" she cried. "May I touch him?"

Bridget nodded. The raccoon regarded Robin calmly and twitched his long thin nose at her outstretched hand. His black mask gave him a wicked look, but just now he seemed mostly sleepy. After a moment he keeled over against the gray cat and went back to sleep.

"His name is Pythias," Bridget said.

Robin thought for a moment. "Then the cat must be Damon."

"Excellent, my dear. Not many children would know that, nowadays." Robin wondered if she meant, not many Village children. "Where did you learn about Damon and Pythias?"

"I read about them," Robin said. "A long time ago. I read all the time when I can get the books. Did the cat really save his life?"

"Oh, many times. You see, Damon is a dog chaser. He found out when he was just a kitten that dogs are afraid of cats that won't run. And he's been chasing them ever since. There are some dogs that come around here quite often, and they like nothing better than to tree poor Pythias. But they're scared to death of Damon. He's broken up more raccoon hunts than I can count."

They both laughed. Robin scratched Damon's head,

and he leaned against her and purred with a roar like a motor. He had a huge head and a smug flat face. You could see why the dogs ran. He looked very full of strength and self-confidence. "I wonder why he likes Pythias?" she asked.

"They grew up together," Bridget said. "They were both babies when I got them. Now perhaps you'd like to meet Betty." They started toward the sheds, but the speckled hens were following so close, it was hard to keep from stepping on them. Robin tried patting one. Its stiff wing feathers made it feel hollow. It clucked hysterically, but it didn't try to run away.

"I've never seen such tame chickens," Robin said. "Why aren't they afraid?"

"Most anything can be tamed if you have time and patience, and I have plenty of both," Bridget answered. "Now here's Betty, one of the most important members of my family."

A white goat with brown and black spots emerged from the shed. Robin had always thought that goats were ugly, but Betty had a delicate deerlike face and her brown ears were neatly trimmed in black. She put her head over the fence and nibbled at Robin's arm. When Robin jerked her arm away, Bridget smiled.

"That's just her way of saying 'hello.' You needn't worry about being bitten. Goats have no upper teeth except at the back of the jaw. I wonder if you would like to help me tether Betty out for the day? Do you see her chain hanging just under the eaves beside the back door? And we'll need the stake and hammer on the bench below it."

Robin ran to the house and was back in a moment. They made their way very slowly around the pens and up the slope of the nearest foothill. Robin led Betty, who tugged eagerly at her collar. When they reached a spot where the grass had not been grazed off, Bridget told Robin how to drive the stake and attach the chain. On the way back, Robin noticed how slowly Bridget moved and how heavily she leaned upon her cane.

"Do you stake Betty out often?" Robin asked.

"As often as I'm able. The grass is good for her, and hay is expensive. Mr. McCurdy sends me some hay now and then, but it's not always enough."

It had occurred to Robin that the situation had useful possibilities. "It only takes a minute for me to get here from the Village," she said. "Could I come every morning and stake Betty out for you? I'd like to."

Under Bridget's steady gaze Robin dropped her eyes. But she really *did* want to help Bridget, she told herself. It wasn't just because of needing an excuse to come often to the stone house. Bridget smiled gently. "That's a very kind thought, my dear," she said. "But are you sure you'll be permitted? Your parents may not want you to be coming here so often."

Robin nodded with assurance. "Oh, I'm sure they won't mind," she said.

They were just entering the neat little back yard when Robin was startled by a whirring noise, and a spark of feathered lightning went right past her face. She blinked her eyes and opened them in time to see an incredibly tiny bird alight on Bridget's outstretched finger. It was a hummingbird. Thimble-small, but confident as a blue jay, it sat on Bridget's finger and cocked its iridescent head.

"A hummingbird," Robin breathed. "It's tame! Is it yours? I wish I had one." There was a fierceness in her voice that surprised them both.

"I see we have interests in common," Bridget said

gently. "But a hummingbird isn't supposed to be owned or given. I'm sure you understand that. I appreciate how you feel about him, though, because I feel the same way. So much beauty and perfection in such a tiny thing. Perhaps you'd like to feed him."

Following Bridget's instructions, Robin found a small bottle of a reddish liquid on a shelf just inside the cottage door. She held the bottle while the hummingbird drank from it. Hanging suspended in a tiny storm of wings, it dipped its stem-thin bill again and again into the sweet-smelling liquid. Watching it, Robin almost forgot to breathe. Finally it flew away to the apricot tree.

Robin was standing staring after it when Bridget's voice broke the enchantment. "It's almost noon, my dear. Perhaps you'd best go home soon. Won't your mother be worried about you?"

"Oh, not much, They're used to my disappearing." Robin meant to sound careless and gay, but a guilty quaver crept in without warning. In answer to Bridget's questioning look, she went on, "I'm always getting scolded for 'wandering off.' That's what they call it."

"Why do you do it?" Bridget asked.

Robin had been asked that question many times, and she always answered, "I don't know," quickly and stubbornly. But there was no anger or even disapproval in Bridget's question. She sounded intrigued, as if "wandering off" was an interesting and original thing to do. It surprised Robin into really trying to answer, "I don't . . . don't . . . I'm not sure," she stammered. "Everything seems to be so mixed up and strange sometimes—and I just have to get away."

"I think I know just the feeling," Bridget said. "But be that as it may, you'd better run along home now before they get too worried. Don't you think so?"

"I guess so," Robin said. "It's been awfully nice meeting you. And Betty and Damon and Pythias and everybody."

"It's been nice meeting you, too, my dear," Bridget said. "And I hope you'll drop by the next time you 'wander off' in this direction."

It wasn't until Robin was halfway home through the orchard that she remembered about the rip in her dress. She couldn't recall whether she'd kept her arm over it all that time at Bridget's. But it didn't seem to matter very much.

What It Means to Be a Wanter

WHEN ROBIN came out of the orchard onto the dirt road of the Village she met the girl with the black braids again. The Mexican girl was hanging up clothes on a line behind the last cabin in the row. When she saw Robin, she put down the pail and smiled.

"Allo," she said, "I'm Theresa. You wan of thee new keeds from cabin tree?" Robin nodded. "I see your two seesters, while ago. You got lots of seesters?" Theresa's English was easily understood, but it rose and fell with a Latin lilt; the R's slurred and the E's sang.

"No," Robin said. "I just have those two sisters, and two brothers."

Theresa examined Robin frankly. "You don' look like your seesters," she said.

"I look like my mother," Robin said. "She's dark like I am. The other kids look more like my dad."

Theresa nodded. "Anyway, eet's lucky for you, you got two seesters." She smiled ruefully. "Me, I got seex lazee brothers." She motioned to the long line of blue denim overalls she'd been hanging. "My brothers!" She nodded her head toward the closest pair, a rather small one with ragged knees. "Thees wan is Francisco, and Juan and Julio and thees leetle tiny wan is Lupe (he's pretty cute) and Carlo, and," she stopped and made a face, "that beeg sloppy wan on the end is José, my beegest brother."

Robin laughed and curtsied to the line of overalls. "How do you do," she said. "I'm Robin Williams."

Theresa grinned approvingly, but then very suddenly her expression changed. "Where you been? You been gone a long time."

"I went for a walk," Robin said, "through the orchard." It was true as far as it went, anyway.

"You better be careful," Theresa said ominously. She pointed toward the hills in the direction of the stone house. "You go for a walk over *that* way and maybe you never come back."

"What do you mean?" Robin asked. "Why wouldn't I come back? I don't know what you're talking about."

Just then the screen door of Theresa's cabin banged wide open and hung lopsidedly against the wall, trailing pieces of torn screening. A large dark woman appeared on the step.

"*Theresa,*" she called, "*ven aquí. Te necesito.*" The woman was fat and her face looked tired, but her voice was low and musical.

"*Vengo, Mama,*" Theresa answered. But as she started for the house, she turned back to Robin. "I got to go now. But you better stay away from that old Palmeras House. Eet's a bad place. And right behind eet there ees a leetle house where the *bruja* leeves." A fat dark haired baby boy had started down the steps of the cabin, and Theresa swung him up in her arms as she went up the stairs. In the doorway she turned and waved.

A *bruja!* What on earth was she talking about? Well anyway, Robin decided, it would take more than a *bruja* to keep her away from Palmeras House, whatever a *bruja* might be.

When Robin got back to the Williamses' cabin, Dad was just arriving from the opposite direction. He had walked over from the mule barns. He looked pale and tired and he smelled of mules. The paleness of his face made the freckles stand out even more than usual. But he was feeling happy because when he saw Robin he said, "Hi, there, Big Enough," and put his arm across her shoulders. They walked up the steps together.

The rest of the family was just finishing lunch, which was just as well since there were only four chairs. Robin poured some water from the teakettle into the washbasin. It was warm, so Rudy must have found a way to mend the stove. Together, Dad and Robin washed up for lunch.

The chipped enamel washbasin was dark blue with white speckles. It sat on a heavy wooden table against the wall. The table had received the splashes from so many dish washings and hand scrubbings that its surface was spongy and full of splinters. You could even pick up little pieces of wood fiber with your fingernails. On the wall, about two feet above the table, was a single brass spigot, going green with age. That one faucet was the only source of water in the cabin. But it could be worse. Many of the places the Williamses had stayed in the last three years had had no indoor water supply at all.

While Robin and her father ate their lunch, Mama and Theda started doing the dishes. Theda washed and made an awful clatter with the tin plates in the enamel basin. Rudy, followed by Cary, drifted out the back door, probably to poke around in the old motor parts someone had left in the backyard. Shirley had been put down for her nap in the other room.

Mama brought a stack of tin plates over to the table. She shuffled them from the top to the bottom of the stack as she dried.

The plates got several dryings each as Mama chatted about what she had done all morning and what she was going to do.

"You know, Paul," she said, "I think we can fix this little house up so it won't look so bad at all. Now that we can count on a steady salary, even if it is just fifty a month, we can put a little bit by for furniture and curtains and . . ."

"Wait a minute, Helen," Dad interrupted. "Don't forget, Mr. McCurdy only said *maybe* it would be permanent. I have to prove I'm able to give satisfaction. Of course, I expect to if I can just keep from getting sick again, but . . ."

"I'm just sure you're going to stay well here, Paul," Mama said. "The climate's so mild and all. Why I wouldn't be surprised if in a few months you had a foreman's job, and we'll all be living in a nice little white house like that one of Mr. Criley's."

Robin sighed. It would be wonderful to believe in Mama's prediction. But it had been a long time since she had counted on Mama's plans coming true. She just couldn't see how Mama could go on believing in them herself. When Robin was little, she had loved Mama's stories about wonderful things that had happened or were going to happen. She couldn't recall just when she'd begun to realize that Mama remembered only the best parts of things and planned things that weren't ever going to happen.

Nobody said anything for a few minutes, and then Mama went on. "Well anyway, Theda and I really gave this old place the scrubbing of its life this morning. Didn't we, Theda?" Robin could see that the rough board floors were still water-logged. "And then I helped Theda wash her hair and set it, and we did some unpacking . . ." At that point Mama broke off suddenly and frowned at Robin. "And Paul," she interrupted herself, "you just have to talk to Robin about 'wandering off.' She was gone again—all morning! And we certainly could have used her help."

Dad sighed and looked at Robin. "Where did you find to go this time?" he asked.

"I just walked through the orchard up to the foothills," Robin said, "and Dad, I met a woman who lives in a stone house that looks like something out of a fairy tale. She was awfully nice, and she showed me her family. At least she called them her family, but they were really a cat and a raccoon and a goat and a hummingbird. And Dad, she's sort of crippled and she has to stake Betty—that's the goat— out on the hills every day, and I said I'd come over and help her sometimes. Is that all right?"

Dad shook his head in helpless wonder. "I never should have asked," he said. "Sometimes when I'm not so tired, we'll go over that again and see if I can make heads or tails out of it. In the meantime, you stay home and help your mother." Dad's voice sounded cross, but his eyes weren't. Robin let her smile say that she knew he wasn't really angry.

"Dad," Theda broke in, "now that you have a job, couldn't I have just a little money for curlers? I just have a few left. I never did find all of them that time Cary used them on that stray dog's hair so he could sell it for a poodle." She turned around to display the back of her head.

Her lightish no-particular-color hair was done up on rags at the back of her head, instead of on the metal cylinders that clustered around her face. She put her arm around Dad's neck and her cheek against his. "I'd only need about a quarter."

"Oh, Theda!" Robin said. "That's all you ever think about. Clothes and make-up and stuff. You're always wanting something for yourself. Don't be so selfish."

Theda looked surprised, but Dad's reaction surprised everyone. "Now that's enough, Robin!" he said, and this time his eyes were cross, too. "I've never worried about the things Theda wants. They're not extravagant. You're the one who worries me. You're the real wanter in this family."

For a moment Robin stared at her plate feeling her cheeks getting hot. Then she got up quickly, leaving part of her beans and bread uneaten, and went into the other room. She threw herself down on the bed. Dad almost never scolded her, particularly not in front of Mama and Theda. And besides, it wasn't fair. She never talked about wanting anything. What did he mean when he called her a wanter?

She lay on the bed for what seemed a long time, but no one came in to see what she was doing. From the other room she could hear Mama telling Dad what groceries to buy when he rode into town with Mr. Criley. The only other sound was deep breathing from the corner of the room where Shirley was asleep on her old crib mattress on the floor.

After a while Robin began to feel less hurt and more curious. It was strange the way Dad always knew what she was thinking, almost before she knew herself. When she let herself really think about it, Robin had to admit that she knew what Dad meant. She just hadn't thought of it that way before. But there were uncomfortable hollows, empty except for vague longings—like when you're hungry but not for anything you can have. And that was wanting, all right, wanting, wanting—wanting.

And Dad must have known about it. It was like that with Dad and Robin. Once, a long time ago, Robin had overheard a conversation between Dad and another man. The man had mentioned, as lots of people did, that all the Williams children looked a lot like their father. All, that is, except Robin, who obviously took after her mother. But Dad had said, "Yes, Robin escaped the towhead and freckles, but in many ways she's the most like me of them all."

That had been a long time ago, back in Fresno, before Dad had had pneumonia and had lost the house and his job. Robin had been pretty young when she overheard the conversation, but even then she had known just what Dad meant. The same things mattered to Dad and to her, important things like books and music. But in the last few years that had all changed.

Gwendolyn McCurdy

ROBIN WANTED to ask about going to Bridget's again that evening after dinner, but she didn't want the others to hear, and the little two-room cabin was just too full of Williamses. Besides, Dad was tired. When Robin asked him to go for a walk with her, he brushed her off with, "Some other time, Robin. I'm just too tired."

So when bedtime came, Robin resolved to wake up early the next morning and walk part way to the mule barns with him. She could ask him on the way. As she climbed into bed, she tried setting an internal alarm clock by saying over and over again, "Wake up at six—wake up at six." She'd tried it before, and it worked, sometimes.

Theda must have forgotten what Robin had said to her when she had asked for curlers. At least, she didn't seem to be angry. As they were getting into bed, she gave Robin her choice, as usual. "Shall we curl up first, or stretch out?" she asked. This time Robin chose to curl up first.

Three years before, when Theda and Robin had first

39

started sharing a folding cot, it had not been so bad; but now they were both bigger. So they had worked out a system. A folding cot is much too narrow for two to sleep side by side, so they each took an end. Part of the night they curled up tight, leaving half the bed for the other person. Then, when their knees started aching to be straightened out, they turned on their sides so the other's legs could stretch out.

In spite of everything, Robin overslept the next morning, so there was nothing to do, she decided, but go to Bridget's and get back very quickly so she wouldn't be missed. After breakfast, Mr. Criley came in the truck to get Rudy. They were going to the highway to get the Model T and haul it to the Williamses' cabin. Robin went out to watch Rudy off, and then she just stayed outside. After Theda and Shirley went back in, Robin started easing away from the house. She was pretty good at that sort of thing. It was just a matter of looking innocently busy at something— like maybe hitting a rock with a stick—while you edged closer and closer to the point where it was safe to make a run for it.

Robin had knocked her rock clear out in front of the next cabin and had started after it when suddenly, from somewhere quite close, a voice said softly, "Robin's 'wandering off' again."

It was Cary's voice, but she couldn't see him anywhere. "Shh!" she said. "Where are you?"

"Here, under the house."

Robin got down and looked, and there he was, stretched out in the dust behind a clump of sickly-looking weeds. He was looking at a book. At least it was part of a book. It must have been in someone's bonfire, because the cover was missing and the outer pages were charred.

"I won't say it any louder," Cary said, "if you'll tell me some words." Cary was always after Robin to tell him words. He hadn't been to school much because there had been so much moving since he was old enough to go. But Cary wanted to read, and nobody ever stopped Cary from doing anything he really wanted to do. His system was to go through every bit of reading material he could get his hands on and underline every word he didn't know. Then he cornered someone, usually Robin, because she was the best reader, and made that person tell him all the underlined words. Robin had to admit he hardly ever had to be told twice.

But the half-burned book was an old almanac, and there were lots of big words. Cary insisted that Robin pronounce each word slowly and then wait for him to say it over after her. His homely little speckled face was puckered with concentration, and he whispered each word fiercely as if he could threaten himself into remembering. Robin felt a grudging admiration. Feeling the way she did about books, she couldn't help but understand, in spite of her impatience. But with all the hard place names, and words like "population" and "agriculture," it took a long time to go through the three pages that Cary had underlined.

When he finally repeated the last word, Robin jumped up and started off across the yard. Any minute now someone would be calling her from inside the cabin. But Cary called after her softly, "Will you tell me some more when you come back?"

"Maybe."

"Robin!"

She stopped and looked back. 'Shh!" she said. "What is it?" But she saw the wicked blue flicker in his eyes and knew what was coming next. He was going to threaten to tell on her again. "All right!" she said angrily. "All right, I promise." Cary crawled back under the house, and Robin was finally off down the Village road.

In the orchard she ran as fast as she could go. She came to the wall, climbed over it, and stopped only a second to look at the big stone house. When she reached Bridget's cottage, she was out of breath. She stood for a minute at the gate, slowing her breathing and looking at the bright flowers and the dark richness of the soil. You would think that dirt was just dirt, but how different Bridget's looked from the hard-packed, dust-blown soil of the Village. She walked around to the back of the cottage and knocked.

Bridget didn't ask any questions when Robin explained that she was in a hurry. She only thanked her for coming and watched, smiling, as Robin took down the chain and hammer. Damon and Pythias were asleep on the roof of Betty's shed, and Robin paused long enough to stand on tiptoe and give them each a quick pat. The staking out didn't take long at all because Betty seemed to sense that Robin could move much faster than Bridget, and she trotted along so fast that Robin had to run to keep up. When she returned to the cottage to leave the hammer, Bridget was waiting at the door with something in her hand.

"It was kind of you to come," she said.

"It was fun," Robin said. 'Maybe next time I can stay a while—if that's all right."

'I hope you can, my dear." Bridget put the small white package in Robin's hand. "These are for you. You'd best eat them on the way home."

Just outside the gate Robin stopped long enough to peek inside the package. There, carefully wrapped in clean white paper, were three fat dark cookies, lumpy with raisins.

Their sweet spicy odor made Robin swallow hard. It had been a long time since the Williamses had had any extra money to spend on sweets.

The cookies were too wonderful to waste by gobbling, so Robin decided to forget about hurrying and take her chances on being missed. She walked slowly through the orchard, taking very tiny nibbles. They were marvelous cookies, rich and moist and chewy. She was halfway through the second one when there was a sudden thudding rush and Robin jumped back as a black horse galloped right across her path. The horse saw Robin and shied into an orange tree, almost unseating the blond girl on its back.

"Ouch!" the girl cried, jerking angrily at the reins. "Whoa! Oh, stop it!" The horse was skittering sideways and snorting. Robin stood quietly, and after a moment he seemed to realize that she wasn't really dangerous. He stretched his neck, snuffed at her, and then stood still. He was beautiful—high-necked, seal-sleek, and quivering with life. Robin finally managed to take her eyes off him and give her attention to the girl on his back.

Now that the horse had quieted, the girl was inspecting her arm where the orange tree had scratched it. She seemed to be about Robin's age. She was wearing jodhpurs, black boots, and a plaid shirt, and her fluffy blond hair was tied back with a black ribbon. "Look what that stupid horse did to me," she said, but there was no real anger in her voice.

"It wasn't his fault," Robin said. "I frightened him."

The girl smiled. She had a nice smile, quick and real, with deep dimples on each side. "Mirlo's always looking for something to be afraid of." She drew her brows together and looked at Robin with a puzzled expression. Then she smiled again. "Oh, I know. You must be from the new family that just moved into the Village. What's that?"

Robin realized the girl was pointing to the package of cookies. "Cookies," she said, gently pushing back the paper. There was a whole cookie and a half left. She didn't really want to, but she added, "Would you like one?"

"You must have been to Bridget's," the girl said. "Thanks, I love Bridget's cookies. She makes the best in the world." She took the whole cookie, and to Robin's dismay, ate it in two bites. Suddenly she looked puzzled again. "How did you happen to go to Bridget's?" she asked. "Don't you Village kids think she's a witch?"

"A witch!" Robin exclaimed. "That's silly. I think

she's nice." For the moment she completely forgot the funny feeling she'd had when she first saw the foreign-looking stone cottage and the bent woman. "Why do they think she's a witch? Who is she, anyway?"

"She used to be my nurse," the blond girl said, "until she got so crippled with arthritis. Now Daddy lets her live in the old gardener's cottage. She's really awfully nice, and she loves kids. It's too bad the Village kids are all afraid of her." She smiled at Robin. "Most of them, that is." She crossed one booted leg over the flat English saddle and leaned her elbow on her leg. Putting her chin in her hand, she just looked at Robin. It was a friendly look, but it lasted too long to be comfortable. After awhile the girl said, "I'm Gwen McCurdy. Who are you?"

"I'm Robin Williams," Robin said, allowing a small smile.

The girl smiled back. Then she cocked her head and surveyed Robin critically. "You know something?" she said. "You're really pretty. At least you could be. You have terrific eyelashes—just like Hedy Lamarr's. I wish mine were like that," she wrinkled her nose in disgust, "instead of short and blond. You ought to do something to your hair though . . ."

Robin felt her cheeks get hot, and although she tried to stop it, her hand went to her straight dark hair. She turned quickly and started off towards the Village. In a moment there were hoofbeats, and the black horse was walking beside her.

"I'm sorry," Gwen said. "I didn't mean to make you angry." They walked on side by side. Robin kept her head down, watching her own bare feet and the high proud steps of the horse. "Look! Would you like a ride home?"

Robin stopped almost in mid-step. Pride was important,

but some things were more important. "Come on," Gwen said, leaning down, "give me your hand."

A few minutes later Mama and Theda and Shirley crowded to the door of the cabin in time to see Robin swing down from the back of a dancing black horse. As the horse pranced away sideways, the girl on his back held him in long enough to wave and call, "Good-by Robin, see you later."

"Good-by Gwen," Robin called back.

Mama and Theda and Shirley were speechless with amazement, but not Cary. As Robin started up the steps of the cabin, Cary crawled out from under it holding up his half-burned book. "You promised," he said.

A Mysterious Gift

WHEN ROBIN went to Bridget's the next day, she had permission to go there. The evening before she had finally managed to talk it over with Dad; and just as she had expected, he had been very sympathetic. "Yes, I think that would be a very nice thing for you to do, Robin," he said. "I'm glad you thought about it. Sometimes lately you've been too wrapped up in your own little world. You need to see that other people have problems, too."

So when Bridget asked Robin in for tea, she was able to say yes. The inside of the cottage was as unusual as the outside. A lean-to addition along the back was divided into a small entryway, a closet, and a small bathroom; but all the rest of the cottage was just one large room. The inside walls were paneled part way up with smooth dark wood. The paneling ended in a little ledge about as high as Robin's head, and above that there was gray stone, just like the outside of the house. The windows swung out like little doors and were made up of dozens of tiny diamond-shaped panes set in dark metal frames. Because the stone walls were very thick, the window sills were deep and each sill held a potted plant or a vase of flowers. The floor of the cottage was also of stone, but years of walking and scrubbing had polished it to a marblelike smoothness. There was a fireplace with a deep hearth, a quilt-covered bed, a small iron stove, and a few chairs and tables. On the seat of a rocking chair near the fireplace Damon and Pythias were asleep, looking like a fat fur cushion.

At Bridget's request Robin carried some cups and saucers from a corner cupboard to a small round table near a front window. The cups had pansies and violets painted on them, and they were so thin that you could see the shadow of your fingers through the china. They were so pleasant to touch that Robin rearranged them several times on the white tablecloth, handling them very carefully. Then, while Bridget held the teapot, Robin worked the handle of the pump that was right on the end of the wooden sink board. She had seen pumps before, but always outdoors, never right inside the house.

There were several other things to do while the water heated. Bridget filled dishes at the kitchen side of the room, and Robin carried them to the table. There was a tiny glass tray with a matching sugar bowl and cream pitcher on it, a plate of the fat dark cookies, a pink bowl full of dark red strawberries, and a pale blue china teapot with a looping wreath of white around it. Robin moved a small vase of pansies from a window sill to the center of the table. Behind the table the casement window was partly open on the garden, and the morning sunlight added patterns of light and shadow.

"Look!" Robin said. "It looks like a painting."

"So it does," Bridget said. "You've arranged it very

nicely. Now if you'll pour the water, we'll be almost ready."

"I like your house," Robin said when they were both seated at the table. "It's different. It's like pictures I've seen of houses in other countries—England, or maybe Scotland."

"Yes, it would look something like that," Bridget said, "but as it happens, it's an Irish house. At least, it was built by Irish workmen."

"By Irish workmen? Did they build Palmeras House, too?" Robin asked.

"That's quite a long story, and it goes a long way back. But I've heard a bit about it. You see, the present Mr. McCurdy's grandfather was an Irishman who came to California during gold rush days. He found some gold—not much, but enough to buy a fine horse and some fancy clothes and have just a little left over. He was tired of the hard work of mining gold, and he'd heard that land was cheap and life was easy in the south. So he decided to go to Los Angeles and buy some land. But on the way his horse went lame."

Bridget paused, and Robin said, to hurry her on, "I'll bet that happened right here. It must have!"

"You're right. It happened right here at Las Palmeras, which was one of the largest ranchos in this part of the state. It was granted by the Governor of Mexico to the Montoya family in 1829. One wing of Palmeras House was built not too long after that."

"Oh," Robin said, "I saw it. It's made of adobe."

"That's right. And that's where Donovan McCurdy stayed while he waited for his horse's hoof to heal. Only he never got to Los Angeles."

"Why didn't he? Did something happen to him?"

"Yes, it did, but nothing bad. You see, the Montoyas had a beautiful young daughter. Her name was Guadalupe

María Francesca Montoya, but her family sometimes called her Bonita. And Donovan and Guadalupe fell in love."

"Did they get married?" Robin asked.

"Indeed they did, and that's why Donovan never got to Los Angeles. After they had been married a few years, Guadalupe's parents died and all of Las Palmeras belonged to her, and to Donovan. But even though Donovan loved California and Las Palmeras, at times he was homesick for Ireland. So when he decided to build a fine new house, he sent all the way to Ireland for carpenters and stonemasons. He planned his new home to look like a grand house that he had admired when he was a boy in Ireland. But because Guadalupe wanted to keep her old adobe home, it was left standing. So Palmeras House became part Spanish and part Irish, just like the McCurdy family."

"Did they have a big family?" Robin asked.

"No, only two boys, Terrence and Francisco. Francisco was the present Mr. McCurdy's father. And Terrence . . ." Bridget stopped to sip her tea, but when she put the cup down she didn't go on. She sat quietly, her eyes blank and inward looking. Finally she smiled and said, "But this little cottage is all Irish. One of the Irish workmen stayed on at Las Palmeras to become the McCurdys' gardener, and this was his home."

"But why don't the McCurdys live in Palmeras House anymore?" Robin asked. "It's such a beautiful house. I think it's much nicer than their other one—the one they're living in, I mean."

"That's another long story, I'm afraid. You see, Mr. McCurdy, the present one, married a young lady whose father happens to be an architect who designs very modern buildings. A few years ago, her father made the plans for a fine modern home, which they built. That was when

Palmeras House was boarded up."

"But why don't they let someone else live in it if they don't want to?" Robin asked. "Are they just going to leave it boarded up that way for ever and ever?"

"I believe there are plans to make it into a museum someday," Bridget said. "When the right time comes. But I quite agree that it's a shame to let it sit alone and empty for so long."

"You lived there once, didn't you?" Robin asked.

For a moment Bridget looked startled. Then she nodded slowly. "How did you know that?" she asked.

"Well, yesterday, on the way home from here, I met Gwen McCurdy and she told me that you used to be her nurse. So if the McCurdys moved out of Palmeras House just a few years ago, you must have lived there when you were Gwen's nurse."

"Oh, I see," Bridget said. "Yes, I used to live there."

Robin sighed. "That must have been wonderful. Didn't you just love living there? I know I would. Didn't it make you feel . . ." She stopped suddenly, feeling embarrassed. Bridget was looking at her with a strange expression.

"What is it about Palmeras House that you like so much?" Bridget asked.

Robin looked down at her hands. She didn't want to talk about it any more. "I don't know," she said. "It's so beautiful and it looks as if it had always been there and always would be . . . I don't know . . ."

Bridget leaned over and patted her hand. "I quite understand." she said. Her manner indicated that the subject was closed. "And so you met Miss Gwendolyn McCurdy. What did you two think of each other?"

"Oh, she's very nice," Robin said. "She took me home on her horse."

"Really?" She must have liked you, then. Let's see. Gwendolyn is twelve now. You're not quite that old are you?"

"I'm twelve, too. I'm just little for my age," Robin said. "Does Gwendolyn come here to visit you?"

"She used to come quite often when I first came here to live. But lately—well, she's quite busy. But Don and Catherine visit me now and then, and Gwen usually comes with them."

"Look!" Robin shouted. A large gray and white bird had flown through the open window and, just skimming the strawberries, had come to roost on the back of Bridget's chair. At first Robin thought it was a wild bird that had blundered in by accident, but she quickly realized it was very much at home. The bird leaned forward and peered meaningfully at the cookie in Bridget's hand. "Awk," he announced in a demanding voice.

Bridget shook her head. "Daniel!" she scolded. "You're such a beggar. Oh, pardon me, Robin. I'd forgotten you two hadn't met. This is Daniel—another member of my family. Daniel is a mockingbird."

"I know," Robin said. "That is, I know it's a mockingbird. But I've never been so close to—Oh! Look out!"

Daniel had accepted a large beakful of cookie, and with a flop of his wings glided to the floor—not two feet from where Damon was awakening with a humped-backed stretch. "Look out! Damon will catch him."

But Bridget did nothing at all. "Watch," she said. Damon finished a white-fanged yawn and leaped lightly to the floor. Robin gasped. It took a moment to realized that Damon was only interested in Daniel's cookie. Daniel cocked his head at the cat, picked up his cookie, and hopped away. But a piece had broken off, and Damon pounced. The mockingbird quickly gulped the rescued portion and looked back to where Damon crouched, cat fashion, over his captured morsel. Then, as Robin gasped again, Daniel hopped back, and with righteous indignation, pecked Damon firmly on his ear.

"Why doesn't Damon eat him?" Robin demanded. "I thought all cats ate birds."

"Not if they're trained very young," Bridget said. "I waited to get a kitten until I had a young bird to raise with him. Daniel was an excellent cat trainer. He has always had a very strong character."

After the tea was over and Robin had helped clear away, she spent a fascinating half hour playing with Damon and Daniel on the cottage floor. Even nocturnal Pythias managed to wake up enough to accept a bite of cookie, which he promptly washed to crumbs in his drinking bowl. It was as good as a circus, but Robin suddenly realized that if she didn't leave soon there would be no time to visit the big house on the way home.

"I think I'd better go now," she said, shooing Daniel off her shoulder. Bridget picked up her cane and slowly lifted herself from her rocking chair.

"You're going home by way of Palmeras House, I imagine?" she said. Robin nodded. "Wait a moment." Bridget put out her hand as if to stop Robin, but then for a second she stood still, as if she were trying to decide something. Finally, she said, "I want to give you something."

She crossed the room with her tiny slow steps and stopped before a carved wooden chest at the foot of the bed. She called Robin and showed her how to lift the lid and run her hand down the side past layers of clothing and blankets until she felt a little box. Robin lifted it out, a small white box that seemed to be made of ivory. She couldn't see any opening at all, but Bridget did something with her fingers, and a lid flew open. She reached inside and brought something out. It was a large, rusty key. When Robin had replaced the box in the trunk, Bridget took her hand, put the key in it, and squeezed her fingers tightly over it.

"I may be doing the wrong thing," she said, "but I think you should have this."

"What is it?" Robin asked. "What shall I do with it?"

Bridget shook her head. "That I won't tell you. Except that you must promise to keep it a secret. If you can't find what it is for, perhaps it will mean I've made a mistake and you weren't meant to have it."

Search for a Keyhole

WHEN ROBIN reached Palmeras House, the key was squeezed tightly in her hand, and she was so excited that her heart seemed to be bouncing against her ribs. Bridget hadn't said so, but she was certain—well, almost certain—that the old key would let her into Palmeras House. What else could it possibly be for?

In the patio at the back of the house Robin took a moment to inspect the key more carefully. It was larger than most keys she had seen, and the metal was rough and discolored. The handle end was round and decorated with a pattern of leaves and flowers, now partially worn away. It reminded Robin of the ironwork above the gates that led to the palm-lined drive. Spanish! That was it! It looked Spanish, so it must belong to the adobe part of the house instead of the Irish part.

So Robin started at the adobe wing and carefully inspected all the doors and windows. But she couldn't even find a keyhole to try the key in. Boards had been nailed over every door so that the keyholes were not visible. She was sure that Bridget hadn't expected her to tear off any boards. And even if she were able to, it would surely be against the law, so there just had to be a door somewhere that wasn't boarded up. She finally gave up on the adobe wing and tried the rest of the house, but with no better luck. Everything was boarded up except for the big front doors of the main entrance, and they were secured with an extra latch and padlock besides their regular built-in lock.

She knew she had to be getting home. She'd already been gone much too long, and if she didn't return soon, she might lose permission to go to Bridget's at all. So, reluctantly, she gave up and started for home. That is, she gave up for the time being.

When Robin got home, she found some heavy string, tied it to the key, and hung it around her neck, inside her dress. All afternoon, while she helped with the laundry and carried wood from the woodpile, she could feel its rough weight against her skin. The feel of it made her shiver, like a promise of excitement.

On a trip to the woodpile she met Theresa. "Allo, Robin," she said. "You wanna play when you tru work?"

"O.K.," Robin said. "What shall we do?"

"You got any paper dolls?"

"No, I used to have some, but they're lost now."

"Me neither. Hokay. We play marbles. Julio got lots of marbles."

Theresa's brothers were already using the marble holes in her yard, so the girls dug some new ones in the Williamses' yard. Robin had never played marbles much, but Theresa knew all the rules.

"How come you not know how to play marbles?" Theresa asked. "Don' your brothers teach you?"

"Rudy's too big for marbles," Robin said. "Besides, he never did play much, except building things and making things run. And Cary never plays any games that anyone else made up. He thinks up his own games."

Theresa was hunched down making spansies in the dust with her brown fingers when suddenly she stopped and looked up at Robin. "Hey!" she said. "I see you comin' home again—from over there!" She pointed towards Palmeras House and the word *there* was heavy with significance. "What you want to go over there for? Deen't I told you eet's a bad place?" She looked around as if to see that no one was listening. Then she whispered, "Deed you see the *bruja*?"

"The *bruja*?" Robin repeated. "What does that mean? What on earth's a *bruja*?"

"A *bruja*! A *bruja*!" Theresa said, as if by saying it over she could make Robin understand. She stopped and thought a moment. Then her face lighted. "A weetch?" she said questioningly. "Yes, that's eet. A weetch leeves over there."

"Oh, a witch," Robin said, suddenly remembering what Gwendolyn had said about Bridget and the Village children. "You mean the lady who lives in the little stone house?" Theresa nodded emphatically. "That's silly. She's not a witch at all. She's . . ." Robin was about to tell about Bridget: her kindness, her wonderful pets, the cookies; but suddenly she decided not to. Instead she just asked, "What makes you think she's a witch?"

Theresa shrugged. "Everybody know eet. And Francisco, my brother, he *see* she's a weetch. Weeth hees own eyes. Francisco ees very brave, and he go and hide and watch and he see! He see thees beeg cat . . ."

Robin nodded. "Damon," she said.

"*Si!*" Theresa cried with surprise, as if Robin had suddenly agreed with her. "That's what Francisco say, too. Francisco say that he see thees beeg cat eating from a deesh and some birds eat weeth heem, in the same deesh—and he deedn't even try to eat the birds. Francisco say that thees ees not a real cat. He ees *uno demonio*, a demon. Francisco say so, too."

Robin couldn't help giggling. "That's not what I meant. He's not a demon at all."

Theresa looked indignant. "Eet's true. And besides, that beeg house ees a bad place, too. My grandmother even say so. My grandmother told me a long time ago a leetle girl got keeled in that house."

Theresa took Robin's shocked expression to mean that she was beginning to listen to reason. "Now maybe you stay away from that Palmeras House," she said. She looked around and lowered her voice. "My grandmother say that a something bad leeves in there. She say eet ees *La Fantasma de Las Palmeras*."

Robin tried to get Theresa to tell her more, but she only shook her head. "Eet's bad luck to talk about eet," she said.

But in spite of *La Fantasma de Las Palmeras*, Robin was back at Palmeras House that very evening. With a little talking, she was able to get Dad's permission to bring Betty in, and that gave her the excuse she needed to get away. She'd also found out from Dad what *La Fantasma de Las Palmeras* meant—the Ghost of The Palms. It certainly had a scary sound to it, but Robin didn't believe in ghosts; and besides, if Theresa's ghost wasn't any more dangerous than her witch, there wasn't much to worry about.

The sun was almost down when Betty had been returned to her shed and Robin finally reached the brick paved patio of Palmeras House. There wasn't going to be much time before it got dark. She would have to hurry, but she really didn't know where to start. Where could she look besides the places she had already inspected?

There ought to be a way to figure it out. There just had to be a keyhole, and there must be a way to find it. She decided to sit down and try to think it all through carefully.

The boarded-up well was handy, so Robin climbed up on it and sat down. She pulled her knees up to her chin and started thinking. If you started with the key, which was certainly a good solid fact—a cold hard fact on a scratchy string—you had to expect that there was something somewhere that it was meant to open. And if you . . . Robin's train of thought went off the track, and she just sat, staring. There in front of her, not two inches from her bare toes, was a large rusty latch. It went over the edge of the well covering, and there was something looping through the hole in it that looked like—! Robin leaned forward and looked over the edge—it was! A padlock! She jumped down from the well and inspected the padlock carefully. It was very large, and the pattern of leaves and flowers with which it was engraved was crusted with rust.

As Robin struggled with the string that held the key around her neck, her mind was seesawing between elation and disappointment: elation that at last she had found a keyhole; and disappointment that it was only to a well. Why on earth had Bridget given her the key to a well? It occurred to her that there might be a treasure hidden under the water of the well, but the disappointment was still there.

The key fitted the padlock perfectly. It turned with a grating sound, and the U-shaped bar clicked open. The lid to the well was made of thick wood crossed in three places with heavy metal reinforcements. It was almost too heavy for Robin to lift, but she found that by pushing she could slide it to one side until there was room to look down. By the light of the last steeply slanting rays of sunlight Robin could see—that the well was not really a well at all! It was not as deep as a well should be, and the bottom was perfectly dry. But even more amazing, a sturdy metal ladder ran down one side to the bottom.

Without even stopping to think, Robin was over the side and down the ladder. It was fairly dark at the bottom of the well, but after a moment her eyes adjusted to the darkness enough to allow her to make out the outlines of a door—a heavy metal door that curved to fit the contour of the well. A loop of iron seemed to serve as a doorknob. Robin grasped it and pulled, and the door swung open with a rush of damp air. But there was nothing to see. The door had opened on the deepest darkness she had ever seen.

Robin put out her hand, half expecting it to be swallowed up by the darkness. Then she bit her lip and moved forward one step into the tunnel. Her outstretched hand found the tunnel wall. It was damp, and the surface was rough, as if it were lined with stone or brick. She didn't go any farther.

Instead, she stood there, one step into the tunnel, and almost cried with frustration. Here she was in a secret passage leading directly toward the stone house, and she knew she would never have the courage to go through it in the dark. And if she went home for a candle, she would not be able to come back until tomorrow. How could she wait that long?

Gwen and Robin

It was terribly hard to have to close the tunnel door, climb back up the ladder, and shut and lock the well covering. But her disappointment was almost greater the next morning. At breakfast Dad said, "Robin, when you go to Bridget's this morning, I want you back in ten minutes. I'm riding in to town with Mr. Criley today to pick up some equipment, and I want you to come along so we can get your work permit. Now that you're twelve, you're eligible for one. Pitting season will be starting in a week or two, and Mr. Criley wants every family in the Village to put as many hands in the shed as possible."

"Oh, Dad!" Robin had nothing against having a work permit, but today, of all days, to have to go into town! "Why do I have to have one? I've worked without one before."

Dad frowned. "Only because it was necessary," he said. "It isn't now." Robin could tell there was no use arguing, and really, she knew that Dad was right. She had hated having to hide or pretend she wasn't working if an inspector came around. But Palmeras House and the secret tunnel! It was just too much of a disappointment.

And because she was so disappointed, everything seemed to go wrong. Robin's own shoes were too ragged to wear, so she had to wear a pair of Theda's that were much too big. It was a terribly hot morning, and it was going to be stifling in the cab of the truck. There seemed to be all sorts of things to be angry about as Dad and Robin walked up the road to the mule barns where they were to meet Mr. Criley.

Hot choky dust swirled up from Dad's high-topped work shoes and Robin's dragging feet. Dad coughed, and Robin looked up quickly. The skin of Dad's face looked thin and tight, and a sharp stab of worry made Robin angrier than ever. Not at Dad—not really—but at the aching fear that so often hit her when she was thinking about Dad. Robin glanced around her, but of course there wasn't a chance of wandering off right then. So she pushed the thought aside and went back to being angry at Mr. Criley.

"I don't see why Mr. Criley should care how many people from the Village work in his old pitting shed," she said sulkily. "He can always get more temporary people than he can use just by going down to the labor office. I mean people like we used to be, before you got this job."

Dad's smile looked tired. "Well, Robin, the way I figure it is that if a man's family didn't work, they'd have to pay the man himself enough to keep his family going. But Mr. Criley has another reason. He says that fewer fruit tramps he has hanging around the ranch, the happier he is."

It was a relief to have something more definite to feel mad at. "That's a pretty mean thing to say," Robin said indignantly. "I knew that Mr. Criley was a mean man the first time I saw him."

Dad laughed and put his hand on Robin's shoulder. "Simmer down, Robin," he said. "Let's just say Mr. Criley's a pretty forgetful man. From what I've heard, the Crileys were doing a bit of tramping around looking for work themselves not so many years ago." They both laughed, and Robin felt better.

The ride into town in the cab of the truck might have been fun if it hadn't been quite so hot and if Mr. Criley hadn't talked so much. All the way in he explained loudly what an important man he was and how necessary he was to everything that went on at Las Palmeras, or the Mc-Curdy Rancho, as he called it. Dad caught Robin's eye and smiled now and then.

The stop at the city hall to get the work permit didn't take long. The library was nearby, and Dad pointed it out, reminding Robin that now that they had a permanent address she would be able to have a card again. That is, as soon as the Model T was fixed, so they could get into town regularly. Just looking at the outside of the library made Robin lose herself for a minute, remembering the feel of libraries. There was that special smell made up of paper, ink, and dust; the busy hush; the endless luxury of thousands of unread books. Best of all was the eager itch of anticipation as you went out the door with your arms loaded down with books. Libraries had always seemed almost too good to be true. It didn't seem possible that anything as important as a book could be free to anyone—that is, to anyone who had a permanent address.

The equipment that Dad helped Mr. Criley load at the farm-supply store was to be delivered to El Pasto. Robin had heard about El Pasto. It was the part of Las Palmeras that was still really a rancho, because cattle were raised there and a few horses. It was up in a canyon, south of the main ranch.

When they passed the main gate of Las Palmeras, Mr. Criley stopped the truck to let Robin off. She waved good-by to Dad and started up the gravel road past the big new McCurdy house. Thinking there might still be time to get to Palmeras House if she hurried, Robin began to run. But she didn't get very far.

The rolling white gravel and Theda's too big shoes made a dangerous combination. Robin's ankle turned, and she came to a sliding stop on one bare knee. For a minute the twisted ankle hurt so much that Robin thought it must be a real sprain, and the skinned knee burned like fire. She limped over to the side of the road by the hedge and sat down. She had taken off her shoe and was rubbing her ankle when she heard a voice say, "Hi! What's the matter with you?"

Robin turned around, and there was Gwen McCurdy looking through a thin place in the hedge. "I turned my ankle," Robin said, putting her shoe back on quickly to hide the hole in her sock.

"Let's see." Gwen came around the end of the hedge and knelt down beside Robin. She was wearing a white sunsuit with a short ruffled skirt, and her blond hair was tied back with a matching ribbon. "I don't think it's really sprained," she said. "It isn't swelling."

"It's all right," Robin said. "It's almost stopped hurting." She stood up quickly and tried to walk; but it hadn't really stopped hurting, and she couldn't help limping a little.

Gwen looked concerned. "Look," she said, "come on in the house. Then if it doesn't get better pretty soon, we'll call Doctor Woods and have him look at it."

"Oh, no," Robin said. "I don't need a doctor."

"Well come on in, anyway, and wash off your knee. If you let that dirt stay on, it'll get infected. Here, lean on my arm."

Gwen grabbed Robin's arm, pulled it across her shoulders, and started for the big white house. Robin tried to protest. She felt silly, but it seemed even sillier to jerk her arm away. They struggled up the wide front stairs and into an entry hall full of huge curved surfaces and glass panels that glowed with light. Wide curving stairs covered with thick carpeting led upward.

"Do you think you can make it up the stairs?" Gwen asked. "We'll go up to my room. Nobody's home except Carmela—she's our maid. She always screams at the sight of blood. You should have heard her the time I fell off Mirlo."

All the way up the stairs and through an upstairs hall Robin determinedly watched her own limping feet in their scuffed and floppy shoes. A stubborn feeling made her refuse to look around. Somehow the whole thing reminded her of last winter, when Cary had come home dragging a lame and scrawny dog. The thought made her want to giggle, but at the same time it made her mad. At least she wasn't going to bounce around and lick people's hands.

But when they reached the door of Gwen's room, Robin caught her breath in spite of herself. "It's beautiful," she said. Gwen only shrugged.

The room was all yellow and white. Sheer yellow curtains over big windows made the white walls seem washed in sunshine. The low bed had a headboard of white leather, and the spread was white, too, except for three huge yellow daisies. A thick rug of very pale yellow covered the floor.

There was even a small white piano, and a table with a telephone.

Gwen brought bandages and a washcloth from the adjoining bathroom and, without seeming a bit squeamish, cleaned and wrapped the bloody knee. Robin was impressed. She wasn't a bit sure she could do that without feeling a little bit sick. Then Gwen flopped down across the white bed with her chin in her hands.

There was the uncomfortable feeling that someone ought to say something, and it didn't look as if Gwen were going to. "Do you play the piano?" Robin asked.

Gwen shrugged again. "I'm supposed to," she said, "but I don't much. Mother used to play, and she thinks I ought to. I hate it."

"I used to play," Robin said. "I liked it. At least I did then. Maybe I'd hate it, too, now that I'm older." She got up and hobbled over to the piano. In Fresno there had been an old piano that had been Dad's. Robin had never had real lessons. Dad had taught her. He used to say that if he had half Robin's talent, he'd never have given up his music. "May I try it?" Robin asked.

"Go ahead," Gwen said.

Robin touched a few keys. The piano had a good sound, clear and true. A little shiver ran up Robin's back. She sat down and played a scale. Her fingers were stiff and clumsy and, at first, she was sure she had forgotten everything. But she hadn't really, because in just a minute a tune began in her head and flowed down to her fingers. It had been one of her favorites. After the first few bars she remembered what it was—the minuet from *Don Giovanni*. Part way through she stumbled and stopped. The minuet was gone, but there was something else she used to play that was beginning to come back. Slow, dreamy music, beautiful and sad—a prelude by Chopin. It was wonderful to feel it coming back from somewhere deep, deep down. It had been so long forgotten. Robin finished the prelude and just sat, almost forgetting where she was, until Gwen said, "Hey! That was good. I couldn't play that, and I've been taking since I was six. Of course, I only take lessons. I don't practice much. In fact, sometimes I don't practice at all."

Robin got up from the piano. To her left the wall was lined with bookshelves. There were several sets of books in matching covers. She ran her hand over the stiff, shiny bindings. She sniffed. The books had a sharp new smell. "Do you like to read?" she asked.

"Oh, sometimes," Gwen said. "But not much. And not that stuff. Do you?"

Robin copied Gwen's shrug. "I read quite a bit," she said.

Gwen got up and took a book off the little table by her bed. "Have you ever read this one?" she asked. The book was bound in leather with red and black trim. It was from one of the sets on the shelf. On the back it said Junior Classics, Vol. 9, *Ivanhoe.*

Robin took the book, and it fell open to page ten where it had been lying on its face. "Yes," she said. "I've read this one. Three times."

"Hey, that's great," Gwen said. "Tell me about it. I mean, everything that happens, and who's in it, and all that stuff."

Robin sat down on the bed beside Gwen, and, while she turned the pages and looked at the beautiful colored pictures, she began to tell all about gallant Ivanhoe and the lovely Rowena, tragic Rebecca, and the evil Brian de Bois-Guilbert. Gwen listened dutifully at first, screwing up her face in concentration. But after a while she really began to be interested. Her round eyes got rounder, and her mouth wasn't quite shut. Encouraged by the effect of her storytelling, Robin played up the exciting and awful parts. When she got to the part about the madwoman Ulrica, Gwen took a deep breath. "Boy," she said. "That's terrific."

When Robin finished, Gwen sighed. "It sounds great when you tell it, but it took me all month to read those ten pages. I guess it's because I have to read it."

"Why do you have to read it?" Robin asked. "You don't go to school in the summertime do you?"

"No, but I was awful in English last year, and Mother wants me to get good grades so I can go to a boarding school back East, where she used to go. So she said I had to read all these Junior Classics things this summer. When I say I've read one, she makes me tell her all about it. So now I can tell her all about *Ivanhoe*."

"That isn't exactly honest," Robin said, but she couldn't help smiling.

"Don't worry about it. You didn't keep me from reading it, because I wouldn't have read it anyhow. And I won't lie about it. I'll just say, 'I'm ready to tell you about *Ivanhoe* now,' and everyone will be happy."

They both laughed. Then Gwen puckered up her forehead and looked at Robin intently. "You don't have any accent," she said. It wasn't a question, but it sounded like one.

Robin had almost forgotten about being careful and was just having fun the way you have fun with anyone, but now she felt herself stiffen. "Accent?" she asked. "What do you mean?"

"I mean you don't talk like an—like you were from Oklahoma. Didn't you come from the dust bowl?"

Robin got up. "No," she said. "I didn't live in the dust bowl. But I've lived in a Model T for three years. I have to go home now." She started for the door.

"Look, don't go getting mad. It's just that most of the people who travel around after harvest jobs haven't been in California very long. I just wondered, that's all."

Robin stopped. She knew that people asked questions for all sorts of reasons, but something made her feel that Gwen really was just curious—and interested. The first thing Robin knew she was sitting on the bed telling Gwen all about her family and how things used to be in Fresno. How Dad had studied to be a musician but his father had died and he had had to come back home to run the dairy for his mother. How he met Mama, who was very young and pretty and worked as an usherette in a movie theater in Fresno, and they were married. Then Dad's mother died, too, but he couldn't go back to studying because babies started coming along, Rudy and Theda and Robin and Cary. Then there was the depression, and Dad had pneumonia and the house and dairy and everything had had to be sold. Dad had held another job for a little while; but he got sick again, and Shirley was born, and she was sick all the time, too. Finally there wasn't any money to pay the rent, and they'd heard about jobs in the crops in the Sacramento Valley. So they'd packed everything in the Model T and headed north. And that's the way it had been ever since.

"Gee!" Gwen said. "That's too bad. But some of it sounds like fun. I mean camping out and all."

Robin didn't really agree, but she said, "Well, maybe. But not as much fun as when you do it because you want to."

"I guess not. Nothing's much fun if you *have* to do

it. It's the same way with reading." Gwen rolled over and propped her feet in their white sandals on the head of the bed. "And I'll bet your mother hated the camping. Mine would. She wouldn't stand for it a minute."

Robin was surprised to see that Gwen was serious. She didn't seem to see that what she'd said was funny. It was like saying that her mother wouldn't stand for earthquakes. "I don't know whether Mama hates it or not," Robin said. "I don't think she believes it, really. Mama thinks everything turns out the way it does in the movies. She always thinks everything's going to be all right in a day or two."

There was the sound of footsteps in the hall, and the door was opened by a tall woman with short blond hair. She was wearing white gloves and a big round hat. Gwen said, "Hi Mom," without even looking around. The woman said hello and smiled at Robin, but it was a rather short smile.

"Gwen," she said. "I've asked you not to sit on your bed."

Robin stood up quickly. Gwen said, "I'm not sitting on it. I'm lying on it," but she got up and sat down in a chair.

Mrs. McCurdy smoothed the wrinkles out of the white spread and then stooped to look in the mirror of Gwen's vanity table. She patted her hair and adjusted the big hat. Then she stood up and just looked at Gwen and Robin. "Well," she said at last, "I don't believe we've met. Gwen, I think an introduction is in order."

Gwen sighed and stood up. "Mom, this is Robin Williams. Robin, I'd like you to meet my mom."

"How do you do, Robin," Mrs. McCurdy said. "It's nice of you to visit us." Her smile was cool and beautiful. "Gwen," she said, "would you come with me. I'd like to see you for a moment."

Robin stood in the middle of the room, feeling awkward and listening to the sound of voices from just outside the bedroom door. After a while Gwen came back in the room. She grinned and shrugged.

"I guess I'll go now," Robin said.

"Oh, wait a while," Gwen said. "I want to talk some more. You don't have to go right now." But just at that moment the phone rang. Gwen sat down on the bed again to answer it. "Oh, hi, Bob," she said. "Nothing much . . . sure I would . . . swell, I'll be right over."

Gwen hung up the phone. "That was Bob Walters. He lives in the brick house up the highway toward Santa Luisa. We're teaching Mirlo to be a jumper. The Walters have a practice ring and some jumps. I guess we can talk some other time. O.K.?"

Five minutes later Robin was once more on her way down the gravel road toward the Village. She stopped once and looked at the McCurdy's house. With its smooth curved lines and gleaming glass it looked like a huge hot igloo. Closing her eyes she pictured cool gray walls under sheltering oaks. Then she turned around and began to run again, limping a little on the leg with the skinned knee.

The Velvet Room

ALL THROUGH the long hot afternoon Robin looked for a chance to slip away to the stone house. She found an old broken candle in one of Mama's kitchen boxes and managed to hide it with a box of matches under the bottom step. It would be handy there in case she had to leave quickly. But then, before she could get away, Mama asked her to take Shirley for a walk under the eucalyptus trees to get her out of the heat of the cabin. Shirley wouldn't go outdoors alone to play. Not even today when her hair was hanging around her face in soggy little wisps and her skin looked like wet tissue paper.

Of all the things Robin didn't want to do that afternoon, walking with a whiny baby just about topped the list. So she started off fast and silently with her head down, hoping that Shirley would get bored and want to go home. But after a while Shirley took hold of Robin's hand and smiled a hopeful, worried smile. It really *was* too late to get to the stone house and back before dinner, anyway. So

Robin began making little houses out of eucalyptus bark, and she and Shirley played with them till dinnertime.

That night Robin decided to go to bed early so morning would come more quickly, but it was hard to get to sleep. It was a bright moonlit night, and it stayed warm much later than usual. Most of the Village kids were up late playing hide-and-go-seek and run-sheep-run. Mama and Dad were sitting out in front of the cabin next door, talking to the neighbors, Jim and Mabel Brown. Robin was alone in the cabin, except for Shirley who was asleep in the other room.

After a while she gave up trying to go to sleep and pulled her cot over against the window. Everything was strangely beautiful. The dusty yard with its pile of auto parts looked different. And the rest of the Village, too, seemed less ugly and makeshift. It was as if the whole world had been slip-covered in the strange, soft fabric of moonlight. Robin had never liked nighttime much. She wasn't too brave about the dark, and then, too, things had a way of growing from bad to worse if you thought about them in the night. But suddenly she saw things quite differently. How wonderful it was that day ended—that there would always be hours that were soft and secret and dim to hide things for a while from the hard brightness of day. She sat and watched until it was quite late; then a cool breeze began to blow in through the open window, and she went to sleep.

As soon as breakfast was over the next morning, Robin was on her way to Bridget's. She stopped at the stone house and hid the candle and matches under some dry leaves in the old fountain. Bridget was out tending her garden, but she seemed to know that Robin was in a hurry and didn't stop to chat. So it was still very early on a warm June morning when Robin finally climbed down the ladder in the dry well, carrying her candle and matches.

She was partway down when she noticed a metal handle on the underside of the well cover. It looked as if it would be possible to use it to slide the cover back over the opening. That seemed like a good idea. Then, if someone did happen to come along, the well wouldn't be standing open.

Robin climbed down to the bottom, lit the candle, and propped it up against the wall. Then she went back up the ladder and, by tugging with both hands, managed to slide the well lid back over the opening. Now the only light in the dry well came from the flickering candle.

As Robin stood facing the tunnel door, the beat of her heart grew louder and louder. She reached for the door pull and then stopped, remembering how black it was inside. Clenching her teeth and holding her breath, Robin inched the door open, keeping her eyes on the tiny flame. She smelled the dampness and felt cold air moving around her. The flame wavered, and she caught her breath in a sharp gasp; but it straightened again and went on burning. The tiny light trembled into the blackness, and it became apparent that the tunnel was lined with stone. The moving flame made hundreds of wiggling shadows on the rough walls. Robin bit her lip and stepped forward.

The old well was not very far from the adobe portion of the big house; but to Robin, inching her way forward fearfully, the passage seemed at least a block long. She began to think that she must have passed right under the house and that she was now heading off into nothingness. But just as she was beginning to despair, the tunnel ended in a flight of stone stairs.

The stairs led up and up until they came to what

seemed to be a tiny room with no doors or windows. But the walls of this room were not the same as the cold damp walls in the tunnel. They were warm and had a chalky feeling. Holding the candle closer, Robin recognized the rough surface of adobe bricks. For the first time since she had entered the tunnel, she took a real breath. She must be inside the adobe wing of Palmeras House.

Three of the walls of the tiny room were the same—adobe bricks. But the fourth wall was different. It was made of wood and there was a metal handle just like the one on the well door. Robin took hold of the handle and pulled gently. Nothing happened! She pulled harder, but still there was not the slightest movement. It felt as if she were pulling on a solid wall. Suddenly she was frightened again, and, grabbing the door, she pulled with all her might. Still nothing moved. There was no way out! For an awful moment she could think of nothing but getting out of the tunnel.

She was halfway down the flight of stairs before she came to a halt. If she left now, would she ever be able to make herself come back? It was awful to give up when she had come so far. Robin clenched her teeth, and, even though the candle was shaking in her hand, she turned and climbed slowly back up the stairs.

Back in the tiny stuffy room, she forced herself to stop and think. There must be an answer; if only she weren't too scared to reason it out. There must be some way . . . She put out her hand, and, taking hold of the handle, she—pushed! And the door swung open so easily that she almost fell forward. It was as simple as that.

Robin found herself in a large, empty room. By the dim light that entered between the boards over the windows, she could see that the room was long and narrow and the ceiling was crossed by heavy beams. A few feet to her left was an immense fireplace. The only furniture in the room was a beautifully carved set of shelves, like a bookcase, that was built into a recess on the other side of the fireplace. Looking behind herself, Robin found that she had entered the room through a similar recess, and that the door that had swung open to admit her was the back of a matching bookcase. She pushed the bookcase back in place, and there seemed to be no door at all—only two built-in bookcases, one on each side of the hearth.

The candle wasn't necessary any more, so she blew it out and put it in her pocket. She started across the room on tiptoe. There probably wasn't any need to be so quiet, but she couldn't seem to help it. Not that she was frightened, because she wasn't—only terribly excited. But her pulse was still pounding a little in the hollow at the base of her throat.

At one end of the big room there was a narrow staircase with ornately carved posts and banisters, but Robin decided to explore the bottom floor first. The next room was very much like the first, except that there was no staircase, and the only piece of furniture was a gigantic table with carved legs as big around as Robin's body. Another room, with a red tile floor and a huge fireplace with a dome-shaped oven built right into the hearth, had unmistakably been the kitchen. Those three rooms made up the adobe part of the house downstairs.

The upstairs rooms were smaller. They had long windows that opened like doors to the balcony which ran all along the adobe wing. That is, they had once opened onto the balcony before they, too, had been boarded up. Except for a huge, heavy chest of drawers in one room and a bare bed frame in another, the rooms were entirely empty. The floors were bare, and there were no pictures on the walls or curtains on the windows. In the empty rooms careful tiptoeing steps echoed hollowly with frightening loudness.

Back in the room with the two bookcases, Robin turned toward the stone portion of the house. At one end of the room there was a large set of double doors. The wood of these doors was not the same as the wood in the Spanish part of the house. It was so shiny and smooth that it felt almost like glass. Beyond those doors the stone part of the house must begin, the beautiful stone house with its tower, its arches, and its strong stone walls.

As Robin put her hand on the doorknob, a wonderful feeling of expectation made her shiver. It was like opening a fat book to the first page or hearing the first exciting notes of new music—a feeling of promise and mystery.

The heavy doors opened stiffly with a shriek of hinges. Sunlight, sifting in long narrow rays between the boards on the windows, dimly illuminated a very large room. In the soft light Robin could see tall graceful windows, a high ceiling, and a floor of shiny golden wood, set in a pattern of little squares. There was a large fireplace with a marble mantel, and the walls were paneled in smooth dark wood. But the room was empty. Somehow Robin must have been expecting that it wouldn't be, because she felt disappointed. Like the Spanish part of the house, this room had no rugs, no curtains, and not so much as a single chair. It looked hollow and lonely.

But it was fun to imagine how it must have looked once. As Robin tiptoed through the room and through the rest of the ground floor, she stopped in each huge empty room to imagine what furniture had once been there and what the people had been like who had talked and laughed and lived in such beauty and spaciousness.

The huge kitchen was especially interesting because, with its sinks and cupboards and counters, it was less empty than the rest of the house. On one side of the kitchen a hall led to a series of small rooms, and on the other side there was a small room lined with cupboards, leading to what must have been the dining hall.

Beyond the dining room was the entry hall, with the heavy double front doors that Robin had inspected from the outside, and a wide stairway that led upward in a graceful curve. At the head of the stairs a hallway ran in two directions. Robin turned to the left and explored a series of rooms that obviously had been bedrooms, although they, too, were empty now. She decided she liked one at the end of the hall best. It was smaller than the others and had a funny little alcove at one end. If she lived there, in Palmeras House, she'd pick that bedroom to be hers.

Back at the head of the stairs, Robin turned to the right. This hallway was shorter and had only one door, at the very end. Expecting only another bedroom, Robin opened the door and stepped into the most wonderful surprise of her life.

From that first glimpse, from the first minute, it was more than a room—more even than the most beautiful room Robin had ever seen. Her hands shook on the door-knob, and the shaking didn't come from fear or cold. Her trembling hands were only an echo of something deeper that had been strangely shaken by that first sight of the Velvet Room.

Part of it might have been surprise, surprise that this room wasn't empty like all the others. But another part of it was a strange feeling, almost like recognition. It was as if she had been there before, or at least had known it was there. As if she had always known that there would be a place exactly like this.

Just inside the door, against the wall, was a little table. It was a rich, red-brown and as smooth as still water. Robin's fingers left a shining trail through the coat of dust that covered it. Using her skirt, she carefully wiped off the dust so that the bright pattern of the grain gleamed through.

A thick pale rug cushioned her bare feet as she moved forward and turned very slowly in a circle. The walls of the room were paneled in dark wood. All along one wall the bright bindings of books contrasted with the wood. The books went on and on, all down one side and across the far wall, on shelves that went almost to the ceiling: except in the center of the wall, where there was a large fireplace with a marble mantel. On the opposite side of the room were four tall narrow windows. Above the windows were arches of colored glass. Sunlight, streaming in through the arches made rainbows on the rug.

Near the fireplace there was a couch covered with a white sheet. Robin lifted it up and peeked under. The couch was of red velvet and had slender curving legs.

The room was full of things, beautiful old things. There were chairs, tables, lamps, a tiny sofa, and a huge square desk with a leather top. At the far end of the room a wide doorway led to a circular alcove. Windows of curved glass lined the alcove above window seats fitted with dark red pillows. As Robin knelt on a window seat and looked out, she realized that this alcove was formed by a section of the tower. Through the curving glass of the window she could look back at the rest of the house—the stone arches and the front entry. And directly below was the driveway and the weed-grown lawn.

It was there in the alcove that she first began to call it the Velvet Room. There were heavy drapes of dark red

velvet at the windows, and the wide doorway that led into the rest of the library had drapes, too. When all the drapes were closed, there was a full circle of velvet. Robin pulled all the drapes shut, and then sat down and looked around.

It was a wonderful, cozy place. A lot of people must have sat there to read in all the years since Palmeras House had been built. There must have been other children who had liked the wide window seats with their deep soft pillows. They probably took their books there and pulled the drapes shut, just as Robin had, and felt safe and comfortable and hidden. If they were a little younger, they probably pretended they were birds high in a nest, or maybe princesses in a magic tower.

After a while Robin went back into the main part of the library and continued her inspection. She examined every piece of furniture, dusting each one carefully with her skirt. The chairs and tables were not like any that she had seen before, except perhaps in pictures. She guessed that they were very old. Near the windows a whatnot case with a curved glass front, was full of interesting things. There were delicately made fans and a row of tiny painted pictures in jeweled frames. There were some Spanish combs with high jeweled tops and two wide silver bracelets with large, blue-green stones. On the bottom shelf were some old blurry photographs that seemed to be printed on tin and some letters with faded, old-fashioned handwriting. Robin decided that the things in the whatnot case must be very special because the door was locked.

Next she began to look at the books. That was only a beginning, because it would take weeks to look at all of them and years and years to read them all. Some of the books looked very old, with their stiff leather bindings and old-fashioned print, but others seemed fairly new. She picked out a collection of fairy tales and went back to the alcove. She opened the drapes a little to let in just enough light to read by and then stretched out on the fat pillows. She was sure she was too excited to read and was intending only to try it out, to see what it would feel like to curl up with a book, as if she belonged there; but the cozy comfort of the draped alcove was very soothing, and soon she was deep in the story of the White Cat.

When Robin finished the fairy tale, she peeked out between the drapes and noticed that the sun was almost straight overhead. She'd stayed much too long. Jumping up, she started for the door; but part way there, she remembered that she was not leaving things exactly as she had found them. What if someone came and noticed the difference? She hurried back to open the drapes, straighten the pillows, and put away the book.

For some reason, it wasn't until then that she really began to wonder about the Velvet Room. She had just accepted it all the way you had to accept a miracle—as too magical for any explanation. But now, as she was preparing to leave, she suddenly wanted an explanation very badly. What if someone came, she thought. And wasn't it likely that someone would? Why would a room be left like this, beautifully furnished and full of valuable things? There must be a reason. And something else occurred to her. Why was the room so clean? Of course, it had been a little dusty, but not at all as bad as you'd expect if it had been sitting alone and untouched for the six years since the McCurdys had moved to their new home. Why was it there at all—a Velvet Room in a silent empty old house? Who visited it and kept it clean? When did they come? As Robin opened the door and stepped out into the empty hall, she held her breath and strained to hear even the faintest sound.

"La Fantasma," The Girl Ghost

ROBIN TIPTOED down the long flight of stairs and through the emptily echoing rooms of the stone house. Time after time she stopped, thinking she heard something, but each time it was only the echo of her own footsteps. By the time she reached the double doors that led to the adobe wing, she felt a little foolish. It was silly to be so nervous. Surely if other people were in the house, she would have heard them.

She opened the heavy doors on their squeaky hinges and tiptoed across the room to the bookcase. There was an awful moment while she wondered what she would do if she couldn't find the way to open the hidden door. But when she ran her fingers up behind the bookcase, they almost immediately touched a latch. She fumbled with it for just a moment before she found how it worked. Then, as she tried lifting up on it, there was a click, and the bookcase swung out.

A few minutes later, as Robin shoved back the well lid,

the rush of warmth and light seemed almost magical after
the damp darkness of the tunnel. She climbed out, snapped
the padlock, and sat down wearily in the comforting
warmth of the sun. There was the big old house, looking
as immense, as strong, and as peaceful as ever. Had she
really been inside? It seemed almost impossible. And yet it
had happened. And because it had, there was a difference in
everything—everything from the taste of a breath of air to
the way it felt to live in cabin number three, Palmeras
Village.

Robin glanced at the sun high overhead and realized
it was almost noon. She sighed and started towards the
Village, looking back now and then: first at the stone walls,
then at the chimneys, and finally just at the tower.

The scolding Robin fully expected for wandering off
and staying all morning was not waiting for her when she
reached home. The Village seemed to be deserted. The
Williamses' cabin was empty, and at first there seemed to
be no one in the entire row of houses. Just as Robin was beginning to feel worried, she saw one of Theresa's little
brothers playing in the mud outside the laundry room.

Juan, or maybe it was Carlo, explained that everyone
had gone to the "peeting shed." Robin was puzzled. She
was sure she had heard Dad say that the apricots would not
be ready for at least another week. She started for the shed
at a run.

Halfway there, she caught up with Mrs. Brown. It
seemed Mr. Criley had come to the Village that morning
and asked everyone who planned to pit to come to the shed
to register and get his first card. Mrs. Brown said she guessed
it was so Mr. Criley would know how many temporary pitters to hire.

The pitting shed was full of people. All the women

and children over twelve who lived in the Village would be working; and many of the younger ones, clear down to the five- and six-year-olds, would be "helping," the way Robin used to help before she was old enough to have a work permit.

Mr. Criley was putting people's names in a book and giving everyone a card. Each card was on string and was hung around your neck, so that every time you finished a box of apricots the card could be punched by the shed boss. Robin would have a card of her own for the first time this year.

The other Williamses were near the head of the line, so Robin squeezed in with them. Fortunately, Mama was busy talking to the woman just ahead of her, so she only said, "Well, it's about time," and went on with what she was saying. Shirley was hanging on to Mama's hand and carefully looking at the ground. She didn't like to be around so many people. But she'd have to get used to it. Mama wouldn't make her help the way some tiny kids had to, but she would have to come to the shed every day. There would be no one at home to leave her with. She'd get used to it by the time pitting season was over.

Robin tugged gently at a wisp of Shirley's thin, corn-silk hair. "Hi, toots," she said. Shirley glanced up and smiled a split-second smile.

The Williamses had just finished registering when, over the chatter in the pitting shed, there came a rumble of hoofbeats. Everyone stopped talking and turned to watch as Gwen McCurdy galloped up on Mirlo. She was wearing Levis and cowboy boots, and a wide-brimmed hat hung down her back on a braided leather cord. She jumped off and, dropping the reins, walked over to the table where Mr. Criley sat behind his big book.

"Hi, Mrs. Lopez. How's Jesse's broken arm?" Robin heard Gwen say to a woman near the head of the line. But then a baby started crying so loudly that, even though nearly everyone in the shed was listening, no one heard just what Gwen said to Mr. Criley. But they all saw that Gwen McCurdy signed the register, and Mr. Criley gave her a card. Glances and nudges were exchanged all through the crowd.

Robin turned and started toward the Village alone. The rest of them could come when they were finished staring. But before she had gone far, there was the thud of hoofs again, and Gwen's voice said, "Well, hi! Robin. What are you doing?"

"Hi, I was just going home," Robin said. She rubbed Mirlo's black nose.

"Look," Gwen said, "I was just going to ride down to the river. Want to come along?"

"I'll have to ask my mother," Robin said.

Mama said yes, probably before she remembered that Robin had been gone all morning. In a minute Robin was up behind Gwen, and both galloped off in a swirl of dust. Where the road ended, they slowed to a walk, and Gwen took something out of her pocket and held it up. "Look!" she said.

"Who's that for?" Robin asked.

"For me," Gwen said. "I'm going to work in the pitting shed."

Robin couldn't think of anything to say except, "Why?" and that didn't seem just right, so she simply said, "Oh."

"It's my father's idea," Gwen said. "My mother didn't much want me to, but Dad says it will be good for me. Mostly I'm not too crazy about things that are supposed to be good for me, but I think it will be sort of fun to work in the pitting shed. Don't you think it's fun?"

"It's sort of fun," Robin agreed doubtfully.

"Why don't we work at the same table?" Gwen said. "Then we can talk if we get bored."

"O.K." Robin knew you couldn't work very fast if you talked much, but she wanted to work with Gwen, anyway, if she could.

The river was mostly dry at this time of year, but it was still an interesting place to explore. You had to cross several yards of sandy, rocky soil to get to the water.

Robin and Gwen left Mirlo tied to a willow at the edge of the river bed. They went on on foot, stopping now and then to look at animal tracks in the sandy patches. Robin showed Gwen how to catch a doodle bug by breathing into its hole, and Gwen found a skunk's footprints which looked like little handprints in the sand.

When they came to the river, they found that it was only a few feet wide and ankle-deep, so they decided to take off their shoes and stockings and wade downstream for a way. In the calm eddies, water scooters zipped away to hide and dragonflies hovered on tinsel wings.

After a while Gwen said, "Look, there's the island." They had come to a little wooded knoll, which in the winter time must have been surrounded by deep rushing water. But now you could almost step across the stream that flowed on each side of it. A little sandy beach sloped down to the water beneath the shade of willows and cottonwoods. The girls sat down on the cool sand.

"This is a nice place," Robin said. "Do you come here often?"

"Pretty often," Gwen said. "It used to be sort of my secret place when I was little. I came here once in the spring when the water was still pretty high. I rode Mirlo over; and the water came clear up to his stomach, and he almost fell with me."

"That's funny," Robin said.

"What is?"

"That you had a secret place. I always had one. Lots of different ones in the different places we've been. Some places we've been I've found real good ones. But I wouldn't have thought that you'd have one."

Gwen smiled and shrugged. She rolled over and started drawing pictures in the sand with her finger. Robin sat staring at the water. She was thinking of the most wonderful secret place anyone had ever had. It occurred to her that Gwen probably knew all about the Velvet Room. If only she could think of a way to ask some of the questions that were bothering her. But Gwen began talking about something else.

"After that time I rode Mirlo over here, I didn't get to go riding again for a month."

"How come?" Robin asked.

"Well, I'd been warned to stay away from the river during the rainy season, but it didn't look very deep so I decided to cross anyway. But when I got home, Mirlo was still wet, and Dad found out where I'd been. Dad doesn't get mad very often, but he sure was that time. He said if Mirlo had fallen with me, there'd be another girl ghost at Las Palmeras."

"Another girl ghost?" Robin asked.

"Haven't you heard about our ghost yet?"

"Well, I did hear something," Robin said, "but not very much. Do they call it *La Fantasma de Las Palmeras?*"

"Yep," Gwen said. "That's our ghost. It sounds spooky, doesn't it? But really, it isn't a very exciting ghost. I don't think anyone ever saw it. We used to hear it though, sometimes, when we lived in Palmeras House. It used to scare Carmela to death."

"Why did you call it a girl ghost?" Robin asked.

"Because it's supposed to be one. It's supposed to be the ghost of a girl about our age, or a little older, I guess, who disappeared from Las Palmeras a long time ago. Her name was Bonita McCurdy. She was my father's cousin, but he was just a baby when she disappeared."

Robin was fascinated. She was learning some of the things she wanted to know without even asking. "What do you suppose happened to her?"

"Well, the police said she drowned here in the river, and her body was washed out to sea. The river was in flood, and they found her horse the next day with a wet saddle. But some people thought she just ran away, or maybe was kidnaped. There was an old Mexican woman who went around saying that she was dead and her ghost was going to come back to haunt the rancho. Then there's this funny wailing noise in the adobe part of the house. We didn't hear it very often, but Carmela was sure it was *La Fantasma*."

Just thinking about it made Robin's scalp feel tight on the back of her head. What if she'd heard it when she was right in the middle of the tunnel? "It must have been exciting, living in a house that was supposed to be haunted," she said, hoping to keep the conversation on Palmeras House.

Gwen shrugged. "By the time I was born, not too many people believed in ghosts any more. But when my Dad was little, all the workers on the ranch used to be afraid."

It occurred to Robin that Bridget had told her something about someone named Bonita. "Did you say the girl who disappeared was named Bonita McCurdy?" she asked.

"Wasn't she the Spanish girl who married the first Mc-Curdy who came to Las Palmeras?"

"How did you know about that?" Gwen asked.

"Bridget was telling me about it."

"Oh, yes," Gwen said, "Bridget likes to talk about the history of Las Palmeras. Dad says she's more interested in the history of the McCurdy family than the McCurdys themselves. But this girl, the one who disappeared, wasn't that Bonita. That first one was only nicknamed Bonita. She really had a long Spanish name that I never can remember. The one who disappeared was her granddaughter."

"And she was your father's cousin?"

"Yes," Gwen said. She seemed pleased that Robin was so interested. "And my father was living right there in Palmeras House when it happened."

"What did Bonita's parents do when she disappeared?" Robin asked.

"Her parents both died before it happened," Gwen answered. "Her mother died when she was just a little baby and her father was killed in an accident on a horse not long afterward. So she just lived with her grandfather until he died. My grandparents were living there when she disappeared."

"Golly," Robin said. "That's the most mysterious thing I ever heard of. Imagine someone just disappearing like that. Right into the thin blue air."

My dad doesn't think she drowned," Gwen said. "He says maybe she'll come back some day. I think that's one reason he doesn't want to tear down Palmeras House."

"Tear it down!" Robin said aghast. "They aren't going to, are they?"

"Oh no," Gwen said. "My mother thinks it would be a good idea. But Dad says it's going to be a museum someday."

"Why does he want it to be a museum?"

"Well, Dad belongs to this county historical society. It's just a bunch of people who are crazy about all the old things around Santa Luisa. The older a thing is the better they like it. And the adobe part of Palmeras House is one of the oldest places in this part of the state. Dad wants it to be a museum of the early days in California. He already has a room full of old things that belonged to the McCurdy and Montoya families."

"Does he keep the things there—in the old house?" Robin asked thoughtfully.

"Yes," Gwen said. "When we moved out of Palmeras House, he had a lot of the best old things put in the library. He says that when the depression is over, maybe the county will fix up the other rooms and the house will be a museum."

"Does he ever go over there, to the library, I mean?"

"Well, not much. Once or twice a year he has some of the women go over and clean everything, and he usually goes over then and looks around." Gwen laughed. "Carmela hates to go because she's afraid of the ghost." All of a sudden she jumped up. "Hey," she said, "we sure talk a lot. Last time we just talked about your family, and now we're just talking about mine. Let's do something else. I know a place where we can catch tadpoles."

That night, for the second time in a row, Robin had trouble going to sleep. She finally dropped off, only to waken again and again. She found her mind still sifting all the fantastic things she had heard and seen. After a while parts of dreams began to get mixed up with remembering, until it was hard to tell them apart.

In the dreams, Robin was back in Palmeras House wandering from room to room. Part of the time she was just Robin in a faded cotton dress and bare feet, moving through rooms that were empty and deserted. But now and then she seemed to be wearing a long dress with a heavy satin skirt, and all the rooms were full of lovely furniture and many dimly seen people who nodded and smiled at her as she passed.

Velvet Days

WHEN BRIDGET opened the cottage door to Robin's knock the next morning, she threw up her hands in surprise. "Don't say a word," she said. "I can guess. You've found how to use the key."

Robin nodded happily. Bridget shook her head very slowly from side to side, but she was smiling. "I should have known it wouldn't take you long," she said. "You know, Robin, I've worried about giving you that key. I did it on an impulse, and afterward I wasn't at all sure it was a wise thing to do. But I think, now, that it was all right. You should smile that way more often. It's not right for a child your age to be so solemn."

Robin could understand why Bridget might have worried. "Oh, I'll be awfully careful," she assured her. "I won't hurt anything or forget to close the well or anything. I promise. And thank you, thank you very much."

"Hush now," Bridget said. "You've already thanked me, my dear. Just be careful that you don't spend so much time there that your parents worry."

"I won't," Robin promised. "They'll just think I'm here with you. That's what they thought yesterday."

She picked up Betty's chain and started for the shed, but then turned back. "Oh, I wanted to ask you," she said, "that is . . . I was wondering if . . . did Mr. McCurdy give you the key to the tunnel?"

Bridget hesitated for a minute, but then she smiled. "Why, yes—that *is* true. It was Mr. McCurdy who gave the key to me."

When Betty was staked out on a fresh patch of dry golden hillside, Robin headed for Palmeras House at a run.

The tunnel was just as long and dark as it had been the day before, and in a way, it was even more terrifying. Although Robin tried to push back the subject of the ghost, her mind kept bringing it up. As she groped her way along the tunnel, things Gwen had said kept popping up to the surface. "A girl about our age who disappeared . . . an old woman went around saying the girl was dead . . . this funny wailing noise in the adobe part of the house . . ."

But although Robin strained her ears until they felt stretched all out of shape, she heard nothing. Once the tunnel was behind her, her fears subsided. The big bare rooms of Palmeras House were sad and lonely, but not frightening.

Her bare feet flew soundlessly up the wide stairway, and then she was back in the Velvet Room. It was everything she had remembered, and more. As Robin closed the door behind her and leaned against it, a warm and graceful beauty seemed to welcome her. Here, in this room, she could never worry about the ghost of Las Palmeras. If there was a ghost in the Velvet Room, it was a gentle one.

That day Robin explored the entire room over again,

from the gleaming curve of a chair's leg to the features of the faces in the miniature paintings in the whatnot. There was one face in particular that held her interest. It was a tiny oval portrait of a young girl. The girl in the picture had calm dark eyes, a pointed chin, and a great deal of dark brown hair. Her faint smile had a look of quietness and gentle strength. She was wearing a dress with a high lacy collar. There was something disturbing about the face, as though it were vaguely familiar. Since the girl was probably a McCurdy, it seemed possible that she might resemble Gwen or her father, but Robin couldn't really see any similarity.

It occurred to her that the girl in the portrait just might be the mysterious Bonita, the ghost of Las Palmeras. It was an interesting thought, and Robin squatted for a long time with her nose pressed to the glass of the whatnot case, just looking and wondering.

Next she spent some time with the books. She had decided to start at one end of the room and work her way to the other. Not reading every book, of course—at least not at first. But just getting acquainted, and noticing interesting possibilities. Right away she found some beautifully illustrated copies of the Louisa May Alcott books. It took quite a while to look at all the pictures, so she decided to finish only the first shelf that day.

Finally, when the sun was getting very high and she knew she'd have to be leaving soon, Robin sat for just a little while on the window seat of the tower alcove. Curled up on the velvet cushions, she gazed down at the great green sea of orange trees. Secret and safe in the high stone tower, Robin felt that all the world was far away and not terribly important.

In the days that followed Robin spent some time in

the Velvet Room every morning. She brought a dust rag from home and dusted and polished the furniture, and even the floors, over and over. She spent a great deal of time stretched out on the window seat of the alcove with a book, or sometimes with only her thoughts and dreams.

Some of her favorite daydreams were about Palmeras House itself. She liked to imagine it as it had been—or perhaps as she would like it to be now, if it were her house. The dry mouths of the sea horses would bubble again with sparkling water, and golden fish would glimmer in the pool below. The stone floor of the portico would be scrubbed and polished like the floor of Bridget's cottage, and the huge sloping lawn would spread a green carpet before the entry-way. The boards would be gone from the tall downstairs windows, and in every room there would be beautiful things, just as there were in the Velvet Room.

On several mornings Robin postponed her visit to the Velvet Room long enough for a short visit with Bridget. If Bridget was working in her garden, Robin sat on the ground and pulled up the weeds near the flowers that were hard to reach with a hoe. As they worked, they talked about all sorts of things.

Bridget had lots of interesting stories to tell about when she was a young woman and lived in Switzerland. She had been married then, to an artist. Bridget and her husband, whose name was Eric, had had all sorts of adventures, like taking a trip around Europe on bicycles with hardly any money. Robin thought it sounded a little like the Williamses and their old Model T, except Bridget's adventures sounded amusing and exciting.

Sometimes Robin talked about her family, or about things she had seen and done; but nearly always her stories were about the days before the Williamses left Fresno.

Nothing much had happened since then that she liked to talk about—at least, not until she came to Las Palmeras.

There was one very important area, though, that they never discussed. As if by silent agreement, they did not talk about the key, Palmeras House, or the Velvet Room. After that first day, Bridget never brought the subject up again, and neither did Robin. She didn't understand Bridget's silence, but then she really didn't understand her own either—except that the feeling she had about the Velvet Room was something she could never share with anyone.

It was on about the fourth or fifth visit that Robin made a fascinating discovery in the Velvet Room. She had been browsing through the books and had worked her way up to the top of the first stack of shelves. Now she was using the top step of the ladder that ran along the shelves on a little track. This whole row of books seemed to be about the early days in California, and some of them looked very old.

She couldn't help thinking how much her father would like to see these books. He was interested in California's early history, at least he had been. Her thought brought the usual sharp pinch of worry about Dad, but it was easy in the Velvet Room to shut out worries like that. So she just shoved it away and went back to the books.

At the end of the shelf were several oddly shaped volumes. Some were long and narrow, like ledgers, and some were very small. The long narrow ones were full of records, written in faded old-fashioned script. They were hard to read, but Robin made out that they were dated in the 1870s and '80s and were mostly records of sales and purchases. There were dozens of entries concerning the sale of cattle and hides and purchases of grain and hay.

One of the very small books, too, seemed to be a record of some sort, with dated entries in elaborate, flowing handwriting. The first entry filled nearly the whole page and was dated January 1, 1890. The faded writing in an unfamiliar style was difficult to read, and Robin was about to give up and return it to the shelf when she noticed a signature at the end of the page. It was a single word beginning with an elegantly curly *B*: Bonita.

Afterward Robin didn't even remember getting off the ladder and crossing the room to the alcove. But she must have, because, a long time later, that's where she found herself. But in between, time had not existed at all. At least Robin Williams and June, 1937, had not existed. In between there had only been Palmeras House in 1890 and a girl named Bonita who had lived there then.

The Diary

On Christmas Day Aunt Lily presented me with this
beautiful volume and suggested that a young lady ought to
keep a daily journal. Aunt Lily says that she was taught that
a journal, faithfully kept, is not only a useful record, but a
valuable discipline in orderliness and organization. She was
kind enough to show me her diary and it is, indeed, very
neat and impressive. She writes a lovely hand and everything is beautifully organized. By making daily entries she
keeps track of all sorts of useful information, such as when
the rugs were beaten and who has been on the guest list for
dinner recently.

My dearest friend, Mary Ortega, keeps a diary too.
However, it's not a bit like Aunt Lily's. Mary's journal
hasn't any records at all, but instead, it is full of her favorite
poetry, confidential observations about all her friends, and
other comments of a very philosophical nature.

I don't have as much imagination as Mary has, and I'm afraid I'll never be as well organized as Aunt Lily is, so I might as well just begin writing and see how it turns out.

I'll begin with some events of the past week.

The day before Christmas, Uncle Francisco and Aunt Lily and their darling baby boy arrived by train to spend the holidays. Grandpa was not well enough to go, so I was allowed to go to the station to welcome them. Of course, Tomás drove the buggy and Grandpa insisted on María's accompanying me, but I was in charge of the expedition.

Uncle Francisco visited us last summer, but Aunt Lily has not been to Las Palmeras for a long time; and it was the first time that Grandpa and I had seen the baby.

Little Donie is almost two years old and I'm sure that he is the most beautiful baby in the world. He liked me right away and spent almost the whole day holding on to my hand or sitting in my lap. I've never had a baby to play with before, except the servants' children, and I find it hard to believe that little Donie is my very own cousin.

Grandpa was feeling better than he has for a long time. On Christmas Day he was even able to come downstairs for dinner and the presents. It was a wonderful time. Grandpa gave me a beautiful silver-studded bridle for Conchita, and I got this diary and two new dresses from Aunt Lily and Uncle Francisco. María gave me a lovely lace mantilla, and Tomás had made me a braided quirt. Of course, I wouldn't think of using a quirt on Conchita, but it does look dashing to have one hanging from one's wrist. I think it was the best Christmas that I have ever had.

Bonita

January 2:

We didn't have our New Year's Fiesta this year. It must be the first time in over fifty years that there has been no New Year's Fiesta at Las Palmeras, but Grandpa just didn't feel well enough. I can't imagine why it is taking him so long to get better this time.

However, many of our friends did made a short call yesterday. The Ortegas drove down from Rancho Venado. Grandpa asked them to stay over as they usually do, but they refused. Mrs. Ortega said she thought it might be tiring for Grandpa to have company in the house. I'm sure she was wrong, but I couldn't persuade them to stay. I wanted them to so much, because Mary and I have not seen each other for a long time, and we have so much to talk about.

While the gentlemen went up to wish Grandpa a Happy New Year, Aunt Lily and I entertained the ladies in the parlor. I would much rather have visited with Mary since she's my very best friend, and I haven't seen her since school let out. But Aunt Lily wanted me to help since she had never met most of the people except at her wedding three years ago.

That brings me to some very wonderful and important news. Last Wednesday Uncle Frank (Aunt Lily asked me to call him that; she says Francisco sounds ridiculous with a last name like McCurdy)—anyway, Uncle Frank told me that he and Aunt Lily and little Donie are going to stay at Las Palmeras indefinitely. I was astounded because Uncle Frank has not lived at Las Palmeras since he went away to school, and I never thought he liked it much here. Grandpa always says, "Francisco has no roots in the soil."

I asked Uncle Frank about his law practice in Los Angeles, but he just said that his partner could take it over, *and that he thought he was needed at Las Palmeras. I really think that is rather strange, since I'm sure I know a great deal more about ranching than he does. Besides, Grandpa has Mr. García, who is the best foreman in the county. However, I'm terribly glad they are staying, whatever the reason. Uncle Frank is so nice, and I adore little Donie. I haven't gotten to know Aunt Lily very well yet, but I'm sure I will now. I would like very much to be like her. She is so beautiful and poised, and dresses nicer than anyone I know.*

Aunt Lily says it's no wonder I haven't very good judgment about clothes since I've had no one but María for so many years. She says Grandpa should have gotten a good governess for me a long time ago. I'm sure it would have been good for me, but then I wouldn't have been able to go to the academy in Santa Luisa, and I've always liked it there so much. I think it would be lonely to study at home.

Besides, María would hate having someone else take care of me; she's been my nurse so many years. I can imagine how she would quarrel with a governess. I tried to explain about María to Aunt Lily, but she only said a young lady of fifteen is far too old to have a nurse and that María should have been sent back to her people years ago.

B.B.

P.S. It's wonderful that there will be so many McCurdys living at Palmeras House again. For so many years there has been only Grandpa and I.

January 4:

I'm ashamed to admit that I've already been negligent about keeping my journal faithfully, but yesterday was so busy that there just didn't seem to be a moment to devote to it. In the morning I rode out to El Pasto with Uncle Frank. He wanted to look over the stock and have things explained to him. He says he's forgotten so much of his Spanish that he has trouble understanding Mr. García.

It was a very enjoyable morning, and Uncle Frank was interested in everything. I'm afraid, however, that he became tired and stiff before the expedition was over. He explained that he hasn't been doing much riding recently.

Grandpa says that Francisco never did like to ride, not even as a boy. It seems strange that brothers can be so different. Everyone says that Terrence, my father, was the best horseman in the county.

Yesterday afternoon the doctor came again to see Grandpa. I do wish he would get well. He's never been sick so long before.

The spring term began today. Uncle Frank is having Tomás drive me to school in the carriage. It makes me feel quite grand and rather silly. I'd really much prefer riding Conchita or going in the wagon with Juan and Catalina.

Mr. Fitzgerald says I'm doing better in Latin grammar. Grandpa will be glad to hear that.

Bonita

January 5:

Today a freight wagon came from the railroad station with Aunt Lily's furniture. So now there is no doubt that they are going to stay at Las Palmeras. Aunt Lily's things *are much newer and more fashionable than our furniture, so she is moving most of the old things up to the second floor and furnishing the parlor and reception room with her things. It looks very elegant but rather strange.*

I had such a pleasant time with Donie today after school. I put him up on Conchita and led him about the patio. He loved it and wasn't a bit afraid. I think he is going to be a wonderful horseman like Grandpa and my father. He cried when Aunt Lily had me take him off, so to cheer him up I took him for a long walk out past the gardener's cottage to the foothills. The grass is getting tall already, and we played hide and seek in it. He is such a darling baby. Except for Grandpa, I love him more than anybody in the world.

B.B.

January 10:

I've been neglecting my diary again. I'm afraid I'll never be as organized as Aunt Lily is. But this time it really was unavoidable, at least in part, because I was away.

On Friday I went home from the Academy with Mary and spent the weekend at Rancho Venado. I had a wonderful time. There's always something exciting going on at the Ortegas', and if there isn't, Mary is sure to invent something. At present she is helping the foreman's daughter plan her elopement. Juana is in love with José Luna from the Blakesly Ranch, and her father doesn't approve. So Mary has planned how they are to elope. It's to happen next Sunday when Juana is on her way to church. We spent all weekend making maps and carrying messages. It was very exciting.

I came home this morning. Grandpa seems to be a little

better. I read to him for a little while, and he seemed to enjoy it.

It rained all afternoon so I spent the time reading. Mary lent me a new novel that I've been eager to read. I think the reading nook in our library is a perfect spot to spend a rainy day. I've spent so many happy hours there.

B.B.

(Robin read that paragraph over several times. It made a funny little tingle go up the back of her neck. "I've spent so many happy hours there," the diary said. Robin could almost believe that if she turned quickly, Bonita would be there, curled up on the red cushions. Somehow, it wasn't a frightening thought. As Robin turned her head, she realized that she was hoping—but the pillows were bare. She went on to the next page.)

January 12:

Father Chadworth came to call today. He went up and talked to Grandpa. When he came down, he said something to me about trusting in God and being brave. I don't know what he meant, but it seems as if he thinks Grandpa isn't going to get better. He must be wrong. Grandpa has had these sick spells before, and he always gets well. And the doctor told me, just the other day, that he was improving.

I've been worried about María lately, too. She has been unhappy and cross. She has taken a dislike to Aunt Lily and refuses to do anything Aunt Lily tells her to do. I don't blame Aunt Lily for being angry, because she's used to ordinary servants. She doesn't understand about María's being my father's nurse years ago and mine since I was born, and being just like a part of the family.

I'm so afraid that María overheard something that Aunt Lily said to me the other day. When we were talking about a governess, Aunt Lily said it was ridiculous to leave the upbringing of a young lady to an old Mexican woman who couldn't even read and write. María is very sensitive about such things, and I'm sure she will find it hard to forgive Aunt Lily if she did overhear. Besides, it really wasn't quite fair, because María can read a little bit, in Spanish.

Bonita

January 13:

It rained again today.

Aunt Lily is having the dining room papered. She says paper is very fashionable in Los Angeles now.

I read to Grandpa this afternoon. He doesn't seem to be much better. I'm so worried about him.

Bonita

January 16:

Still raining.

Juana's elopement is off, at least for now. It was raining so hard on Sunday that her father wouldn't let her go to church.

Grandpa still very sick.

January 20:

The doctor was here again this morning. Grandpa is worse.

The next page of the diary was blank except for a few words written in a shaky, uncontrolled hand. The ink was so blurred and smeared that Robin had to hold it up to the light to make out the words.

February 5:

> *Donovan Patrick McCurdy age 68*
> *died February 3, 1890, at Las Palmeras.*

The diary ended there. The rest of the pages in the little book were blank. Robin sat staring at the crumpled blurry page for a long time. Then she climbed the ladder, replaced the diary on the top shelf, and ran from the room.

Even though she ran all the way, she was a little bit late getting back to the Village. She had promised to be back by eleven, because the family was going on a shopping trip to Santa Luisa. The Model T was finally repaired, and Dad had gotten the afternoon off. It would be the family's first trip into town since they had come to Las Palmeras. Until now, Dad had been borrowing rides when he had to go in for groceries.

When Robin reached home, Theda was already waiting in the car. Theda loved to go shopping, even when there wasn't much money to spend. She could window-shop happily by the hour, or use up half a day deciding how to spend a quarter. When Theda saw Robin, she said, "Well, so you finally made it, after all. I don't see why you like to spend so much time at that old lady's house. What do you do over there anyway?"

The rest of the family was straggling out of the cabin. Robin ignored Theda's question. "I've got to get my shoes," she said. "I'll be back in a minute." She didn't want to get into a conversation. There was too much to think about.

All the way into town, while Cary read the billboards at the top of his lungs and Shirley cried because she'd left her doll at home, Robin's mind was full of the faded flowery phrases of the diary. What happened then? she kept wondering. What happened to Bonita after her grandfather died?

"La Fantasma de Las Palmeras"

EVEN BEFORE Robin found the diary, she was intrigued by the story Gwen told her about the girl who had disappeared so mysteriously. But afterwards it was more than that. It was almost as if Bonita were someone she knew very well and was very close to.

Almost every day when she got to the Velvet Room, Robin took down the diary and read parts of it over again. She spent many minutes peering into the glass case at the tiny portrait. She was sure now that it must be Bonita. In her imagination, she lived the events in the diary as Bonita must have lived them and pictured how all the people looked: Maria, Aunt Lily, Uncle Francisco, the adventuresome Mary, and the baby Donie, who must have grown up to be Gwen's father, Donovan McCurdy the Second.

At first Robin wondered about Bonita's disappearance, but after a while she didn't anymore. It just didn't seem possible that anything had happened to her at all. Without thinking about it very much, Robin developed a rather vague theory that Bonita must have left for reasons of her own; probably an elopement with a nobleman from another country; or perhaps she ran away to become an actress— and under a fictitious name had become rich and famous.

On Thursday of the last week before pitting season Robin went to Bridget's as usual and staked Betty out, before going on to Palmeras House. It was a beautiful morning, sunny and warm but with a cool, fresh breeze. In the Velvet Room she did the usual things. She dusted the furniture, looked through a few books, and then just strolled around, thinking and imagining. She drifted into the alcove, knelt on the cushions, and looked out.

The shiny leaves of the orange trees moved and glittered in the sun. It took a strong breeze to move the stiff compact trees that much, but not a rattle or a creak or even a sigh of wind could be heard inside the stone walls of the tower. It occured to Robin that it would be nice to be there during a real storm, when there was wind and rain and thunder and lightning; how nice to watch the crazy violence of a storm calmly, as if from another world—a safe strong world beyond the reach of wind and rain and everything.

A little later, Robin started home. She went downstairs the usual way and was just closing the double doors that led into the adobe wing, when suddenly she heard something. It came from no particular direction, and yet from everywhere—a faint, faraway wailing, like a distant voice singing a sad song. At times it died away, only to return a moment later.

It must have been close to a minute that Robin stood there as if paralyzed. Her tongue felt dry and heavy, and the skin on the back of her neck prickled. But time went by and nothing happened. The wailing voice rose and fell, but it seemed to get no closer and no farther away. Her

fingers were stiff when she finally loosened them from the
door knob and forced herself to tiptoe on across the room.

When Robin climbed out of the well a few minutes
later, her heartbeat was still echoing in her stomach like the
thudding of a bass drum. Her hands were shaking so
much she could scarcely fasten the padlock. She needed
help. There were some questions she just had to ask before
she went back to Palmeras House. Almost without thinking,
she hurried towards Bridget's cottage, trying to compose
herself enough to think of a diplomatic way to bring the
subject up.

But she didn't need to say anything. Her face said
all that was necessary. As Bridget opened the cottage door,
she gasped. "My goodness, child! What happened? You're
as white as a sheet."

Robin opened her mouth, but to her surprise nothing

came out but a little squeak. "Ghost," it said. "Ghost in Palmeras House."

Taking Robin's arm, Bridget led her to a chair. "Sit down," she said. "Lean forward, and put your head down. You look as if you're going to faint. Now just sit still, and I'll get you something."

Robin did as she was told. She had never fainted in her life, and it seemed as if it might be an interesting thing to do; but as soon as she put her head down, she began to feel quite normal. In a moment Bridget was back with a cup of very sweet tea.

"Now sip that slowly," she said, "and when you have your breath back, tell me all about it."

After several swallows Robin was ready to begin. "I heard the ghost," she said. *"La Fantasma de Las Palmeras.* I was just leaving the house and I heard it. It was like moaning or crying all around me. It scared me about to death."

Bridget looked distressed. "I should have thought to warn you about that," she said. "But it doesn't happen very often, and it didn't occur to me that you might be there when it did. It's really nothing dangerous at all. Some years ago the tile roof of the adobe section of the house had to be replaced, and, since that time, whenever there is a strong wind from the ocean, it whistles across the openings in the tiles: like blowing across the neck of a bottle. But it has to be a strong wind and from just the right direction, so it happens very seldom, especially in the summer. But if you've known about *La Fantasma* all along, you were very brave to go in there all by yourself every day."

"Well, I'd heard about it," Robin said. "Gwen told me about the ghost once, and the kids in the Village talk about it a lot. I just never believed in it. I guess I just couldn't believe anything bad about Palmeras House."

"I wonder why Gwen didn't tell you about the real cause of the sounds," Bridget said. "I know she knows, because we used to talk about it. What *did* she tell you exactly?"

"I guess she just left that out to make it a more exciting story," Robin said. "I mean, a ghost *is* more interesting than some noisy tiles. She just told me that people thought the house was haunted, and all about Bonita, the girl who disappeared a long time ago when Mr. McCurdy was a baby. Do you know about that?"

"Oh, yes," Bridget said. "Anyone who's been around Las Palmeras very long hears about that."

A new thought had just occurred to Robin. "I wonder why they thought the wind noise was the ghost of Bonita?" Robin asked. "I mean, other people died at Las Palmeras. Why couldn't it have been someone else's ghost?"

"Well, as I understand it," Bridget said, "it was due to a number of circumstances. After Bonita disappeared there were all sorts of strange rumors. Even though the police were sure she had drowned, there were people who believed that Bonita's own aunt and uncle might have had something to do with her disappearance. You see, Bonita's grandfather had just died, and to everyone's surprise he had left most of Las Palmeras to Bonita. So there seemed to be a motive."

"Oh-h-h," Robin said, "do you think they really might have done something to her, her own aunt and uncle?"

"Oh no. But it made things look rather bad. And then when the roof started wailing, the ghost story spread like wildfire. It didn't take the McCurdys long to discover what it really was; but in a case like that, there are people who aren't much interested in the truth. I guess the family tried hard to stop the rumors for a while, but no one worries

much about them any more. In fact, the present Mr. Mc-
Curdy told me that he doesn't try to tell people that there
isn't a ghost. Since Palmeras House is standing empty, he
thinks it's just as well if some people are afraid of it. Otherwise there might be prowlers."

"Gwen said an old Mexican woman helped to spread
the rumors," Robin said. "I bet I know who it was. I bet it
was María. She didn't like Aunt Lily and Uncle Frank."

Bridget looked startled. "Who told you . . .? Where
did you hear . . .?"

"The diary," Robin interrupted. "Don't you know
about the diary? It's right there on a shelf in the Vel—the
library, with all the other books."

"Of course," Bridget said, "of course it is. I just wasn't
thinking that you might have read it."

"I read it all the time," Robin said. "Oh—and Bridget
—I've been wanting to ask someone. Do you know if the
little oval-shaped picture in the glass cupboard is Bonita?"

Bridget's answer came slowly. "Why, yes, I believe it
is," she said.

Robin clapped her hands delightedly. "I knew it!" she
said. "It just had to be."

Bridget only said, "Oh"; but her eyebrows made it
into a question.

It was hard to explain just why she'd been so sure it
was Bonita. "It's just that I think about Bonita a lot. When
I'm there, I sort of imagine about her. Sometimes I even
pretend I'm Bonita. It's like a game, I guess. And that's
the way she looks. Just exactly. I don't think I could
imagine her any other way."

That night Robin sat on the steps of the cabin in the
long June twilight, thinking. The rest of the family was
in the house, except for Cary, who kept galloping through

the yard carrying a broken lath and the lid of a garbage can. Once he stopped in mid-charge and yelled, "Hey, Robin! You're the damsel in distress; I'm rescuing you."

"Go away," Robin said distantly. "I don't want to be rescued."

"O.K. for you. Then you're an ugly old witch, and you're rotting in my dungeon." He loosened imaginary reins and pranced away. The next time through the yard he stopped and added, "And you got red eyes and a green nose!"

Robin went back to her thoughts until the screen door banged open and Shirley came out trailing a battered page of a funny paper. She sat down and arranged herself just like Robin, with her bare heels tucked up against the stair riser and her skirt wrapped around her legs. Then she carefully smoothed out her piece of funny paper on the step next to Robin. "Read to me, Robin?" she asked.

Robin sighed and turned her head away. "Not now," she said. "I'm thinking." There was a sound behind her, and Robin looked back to see Dad standing in the doorway.

Robin felt uncomfortable. Finally Dad said, "Have you been feeling bad lately, Robin?"

"I feel all right," Robin said.

He shook his head. "Well, you've been acting like a sleepwalker. You know, I've never taken this 'wandering off' problem of yours very seriously, but maybe I should. Looks to me as if you've 'wandered off' from this family permanently. Even when you're right here at home."

After Dad went back inside, Cary crawled out from under the house. He must have been listening, because he crossed his eyes and staggered around with a vacant expression on his face and his hands out in front like a sleepwalker. "This is you, Robin," he said. "This is you."

Apricots

THE NEXT Monday morning everyone in the Williams family except Shirley became wage earners. Of course, Cary wasn't legally old enough, but he would stand at Mama's table and "help."

Robin awoke at five-thirty that morning, when Rudy got up to build the fire in the wood stove. She didn't go back to sleep because she knew she'd have to get up soon if she was going to get Betty staked out and still be on time for work. She'd have to eat breakfast early with Mama and Dad and Rudy.

She could tell already that it was going to be a hot day, but right now the air was still fresh and cool, and the blankets of the cot were pleasant. Robin put her feet against Theda's warm back and snuggled down for a last five minutes. She could hear Mama and Dad getting up in the other room.

In a few minutes Dad came out, carrying his shaving things. He grinned at Robin and said, "Morning, Big

Enough." That meant Dad was feeling pretty good.

While Mama and Dad were over at the wash-house, Robin got up and put water in the coffee pot and put it on the stove. Then she took her clothes into the bedroom to dress. It was different having breakfast with the first shift. Usually Robin ate later with the little kids, but it was a lot more peaceful this way. Rudy and Dad never talked much, and even Mama was pretty quiet this early in the morning.

Robin and Rudy and Dad left the house together. Dad and Rudy had to be at work at six-thirty. Dad was driving a mule sled. The sleds were used to bring boxes of apricots down from the hillside orchards on roads that were too steep for the tractors. Rudy was on a picking crew. Robin, of course, was on her way to Bridget's.

When Robin arrived at the cottage, Bridget was getting ready to milk Betty. She put a pan of oats on the bench by the back door and Betty jumped up onto the bench. With the little goat up so high, Bridget was able to sit comfortably on a stool to do the milking.

"So, you're starting work today," Bridget said.

Robin nodded.

"How many hours a day will you be working?"

"Well, we may get off a little early for a day or two, till more fruit gets ripe, but after that it will be from seven to five."

Bridget frowned. "That's a long time for a little thing like you to stand at a table."

"Oh, kids a lot littler than I am do it. And sometimes the trucks are late, and we get some time off to play."

Bridget shook her head. "What do you find to think about all that time, while you're working? Do you talk with the other children?"

"Well, usually the shed boss doesn't like you to talk much. It slows you down. The really bad part is that thinking slows you down, too. At least it does me. Pitting wouldn't be bad if you could think about other things. But if you want to earn much money, you have to keep your hands moving as fast as you possibly can all the time."

Bridget shook her head again as she finished her milking. "Well, you'd best run along with Betty, dear, or you'll be late. And stop by for a cookie before you go."

When Robin got back to the Village, the family was almost ready to leave for the pitting shed. Shirley was clutching her rag doll, and her eyes were red. Theda was still combing her hair, and Cary was under the table with a book. Robin couldn't understand why Cary always had to be under things or on top of them. She guessed it was because he just wasn't an in-between sort of person.

Robin took Shirley outside. They sat down on the steps to wait for the others, and Robin gave Shirley half a cookie that she had saved for her. While Shirley ate the cookie, Robin made Annie, the rag doll, jump up and down and say, "Goodie, goodie, Shirley's taking me to play at the pitting shed."

It wasn't quite seven when the Williamses left the Village, but the air had already lost its morning coolness, and smelled of heat and dust. As they approached the shed, there were other smells: the tangy smell of ripe apricots and the biting fumes from the sulfur houses.

At one end of the shed there was a table piled high with pans and knives. Robin picked out a big pan and a knife that had been sharpened until the blade curved inward. She liked that kind best. She looked around for Gwen, but with no success. It would be best not to count on her. It was hard to believe she would really come.

Robin waited until Mama had picked out a table, and then she took one at the other end of the shed. She'd always had to work at Mama's table before, and Mama was forever telling her to keep her mind on her work. Fred Criley, who was a shed boy, put a tray on her table and brought her a field box of apricots.

When Robin picked up the first apricot, her mouth watered. It was always like that at the first of the season. They tasted wonderful for the first day or two, but after that you were sick of the very smell of them. The apricot was still warm from the sun and so ripe that the juice ran down Robin's chin as she bit into it. She wiped her chin on her skirt and started to work.

It was almost fun at first. You filled your pan with fruit from the box. Moving as fast as you could, you ran your knife around the apricot, broke it open, pried out the pit with your thumb, and dropped it into the pan. Then you put the two bright orange halves down on the tray and reached for another. The first few rows looked so small compared to the bare expanse of the huge wooden tray that you always felt it would never be full. But after a long time it was. Then you called "Tray!" and the shed boys came and took it away and brought another. When your field box was empty, the shed boss punched your card, and a shed boy brought you a new box.

That year pitters at Las Palmeras were to receive ten cents for a fifty-pound box. It was better pay than last year, and Robin could remember when they had earned only five cents a box. She should be able to make eighty or ninety cents a day if she kept her mind on what she was doing. Of course, some of the very best pitters earned twice that much, and even Theda could pit ten or eleven boxes in a day. But Robin daydreamed too much.

The pitting shed was a strange place. It had no walls or floor whatever, only poles holding up a roof above hard-packed earth. A track of metal rails ran the length of the shed to carry the little flat cars that took the tall stacks of loaded trays to the sulfur houses. On each side of the track was a long row of pitting tables. Outside the shed, near the road, was an open space where the trucks coming in from the orchards turned around and unloaded the boxes of fruit. Already, this morning, there was a huge stack of boxes, which meant that there would probably be no time off today.

Straight ahead of Robin, out beyond the end of the shed, were the sulfur houses. They were tightly built and had holes in the floor where pots of bright yellow sulfur were ignited. After about four hours in the sulfur fumes, the trays of fruit were spread out in an open field to dry in the hot July sun. At every shed where the Williamses had worked, children had told stories about someone who had been locked in a sulfur house by mistake and came out all yellow and shriveled and dead. But Robin didn't think it had ever really happened.

At the other end of the row of tables Mama was frowning and saying something to Cary, and Robin could guess what. Cary, like Robin, had a hard time keeping his mind on apricots all day. And there was poor scary little Shirley, with Annie still clutched in her arms, sitting on a field box near Mama's feet. At the next table Theda was working hard and steadily as she always did. She'd been impatient for pitting season to start, and Robin had seen the list she'd already made of the new clothes and things she was going to buy.

When Robin finished her first tray of fruit, Fred Criley and Theresa's big brother José put it on the cart.

Apparently José was to be the other shed boy. Theresa always said her brothers were lazy, but Robin soon decided that José wasn't going to get much of a chance to be a lazy shed boy. Fred Criley saw to that. All morning Fred swaggered up and down the aisle or sat enthroned on a pile of boxes and told José what to do. Only when two people were absolutely necessary to handle a full tray did Fred bestir himself.

Mr. Criley was a strict shed boss, who didn't allow any loafing or playing, but he never seemed to notice what Fred did. He even laughed when Fred put a snake in Theresa's pit pan. Theresa screamed like everything, and everyone stopped work to find out what had happened; but Mr. Criley acted as if it were a joke.

Long before noon Robin's legs and back ached from standing. There were two small cuts on her right thumb, and the apricot juice made them smart constantly. On the way back to the Village for lunch, all the Williamses were quiet. Even Cary walked along silently with his head down, like everybody else. Somehow, seeing Cary like that made Robin feel even more miserable. She couldn't think why, though.

She stole another look at him—plodding along with his tousled head hanging—and the aching lump in her throat grew. She explored the feeling gingerly the way you look under a bandage, reluctant but curious.

He'd always been such an embarrassing little pest. Why did seeing him so beaten and ordinary make her feel so—so deserted, almost?

As she shuffled along through the hot dust, she decided that it had something to do with the day the family had arrived at Las Palmeras and Cary had hit Fred Criley with Dad's shovel. She'd had a notion then—for the first time—that she and Cary were sort of alike. In some ways, anyway. Only maybe Cary was braver. Like using a shovel instead of . . .

She was suddenly too tired to think about it anymore, but she did know that she wouldn't like to see Cary change, at least not entirely.

Only Theda managed to be cheerful on the walk home. She picked up dirty, tearful Shirley and carried her on her back. When they caught up with Robin, Theda said, "It'll be better in a day or so. Remember, it's always like this till you get used to standing. Then it's not bad at all."

It really was better in a day or so, and on the third day Gwen came to work. She'd been away on a shopping trip to Los Angeles with her mother. Gwen said her mother had so many things to buy it was lucky they got back before all the apricots were gone. "Don't worry," Robin sighed. "There's plenty left." She pointed to the stacks of boxes, row after row, as tall as a man's head.

To Robin's surprise Gwen turned out to be a good pitter when she was trying. In just a day or two, she was almost as fast as Robin; and on the days when she was interested in pitting she was steadier, so that her best day's record was soon better than Robin's. But on other days she was more intersted in talking. And no matter how much Gwen talked, Mr. Criley never told her to "hesh up and pit" the way he sometimes did the other children. But on the days when they talked a lot, neither Gwen nor Robin collected many punches on their cards.

They found they had many things to discuss. They talked for hours about animals they liked—horses in particular—schools they'd been to, and movies they'd seen. They told about scary or unusual things that had happened to people they'd known. And Robin told some more stories from the books in Gwen's Junior Classics Library. Gwen was a very good listener. No one except Shirley had ever listened to Robin's storytelling with such enthusiasm. Sometimes Robin would tell a story up to an exciting part, and then stop and say that it was Gwen's turn. So Gwen would read a few chapters that night and tell Robin about it the next day. She got pretty interested in some of the books. Once she said, "Gee, Robin. Nobody ever told me about the good things in those books. I always thought they were just for improving your mind and increasing your vocabulary and stuff like that."

Of course, working from seven to five seven days a week left no time at all for the Velvet Room. To Robin's surprise, she didn't even think about it very much, right at first. There was Gwen to talk to every day, and after work Robin was almost too tired to think at all. But during the third week of the season Gwen left with her parents on a vacation trip to Hawaii. Things were very different after that.

In the first place, it suddenly got hotter. Robin had thought it was plenty hot before, but now the east wind started blowing in from the desert, carrying heat and dust from thousands of acres of scorching sand. The fruit ripened so quickly that everyone was urged to work extra hours, and several more temporary pitters were hired. The too-ripe fruit was hard to cut and left your hands so slippery that it was impossible to keep from cutting yourself.

To make matters worse, Robin now began to get her share of Fred Criley's special attentions. While José was busy doing most of the work, Fred found time to torment a selection of favorite victims. Fred smashed ripe apricots in people's hair, put dirt in lunches, and planted snakes

and spiders where they'd be found by someone who was extra timid about such things. As long as Gwen had been at Robin's table, Fred had left her alone. But now he made up for lost time. He smeared apricots on the back of Robin's dress and flipped over her full pit pan on her tray. He took her good knife, leaving an old rusted one in its place, and put a very dead gopher in her box of fruit. Worst of all, he killed a baby mouse that she had just rescued from under a stack of trays.

There was no use complaining to Mr. Criley, so Robin just tried to pretend that it didn't bother her. But after Fred squashed the little mouse, there were times when she couldn't bear even to look at him. She hated him so much it made her feel sick.

She tried to tell Dad about it, but he only said what he always did: not to judge anybody until you knew what made him the way he was. He said that Mrs. Criley had once told Mama some things that sort of explained about Fred. The Crileys had lived on a farm in Oklahoma right in the worst of the dust bowl, and things had been very bad. Dad said that hunger and despair sometimes did strange things to people.

Robin could understand that. She could even feel sorry for the Fred Criley who had been a hungry boy back there on that dust-killed farm in Oklahoma. But how could anyone feel sorry for a big strong Fred Criley who strutted through the pitting shed looking for somebody to torment?

The days in the pitting shed passed slowly and more slowly. As Robin worked hour after hour, day after day, with the dust stuck to her sweaty face, and chapped lips, and the dry wind whipping her hair into her eyes, she began to think more and more about the Velvet Room.

She found that by concentrating she could see it almost as clearly as if she were there. With her eyes wide open, she could make a picture grow up like a wall between herself and her surroundings. Strong stone walls rose up through cool green air. Inside the walls were smooth shining surfaces and deep soft ones. There was no sound or stir, and the air was clean and still.

The picture was so clear sometimes, that for whole minutes it shut out everything else: all the dirt and heat and wind; all the tired dust-colored people; all the crying babies and scolding mothers. Sometimes it could even shut out the flies that crawled up the backs of Robin's sweaty legs and the smarting cuts on her fingers.

At night it was easier. As she lay awake in the hot cabin, Robin could almost convince herself that she really was in the Velvet Room. With her eyes wide open in the darkness she could see it clearly. But it was important to keep her eyes open, because the moment they closed, she could see nothing but apricots, as if the inside of her eyelids had been indelibly printed with row upon row of juicy orange circles.

A Cold, Dark Wind

TOWARD THE END of pitting season Robin finally found time to make another visit to the Velvet Room. The trucks began coming in from the orchards with smaller loads of fruit, and sometimes there wasn't enough to go around. When that happened, the women got what boxes there were, and the children were allowed to go and play.

The very first day that Robin found herself set free, she headed for Palmeras House. It had been a long time. What if the stub of a candle that she had left in the well had melted or been eaten by mice? Perhaps the matches would be too damp to work? She decided, in that case, she'd just have to go through the tunnel in the dark. There wasn't enough time to go back to look for another candle, and, anyway, she wasn't afraid of the tunnel any more. At least, not much.

However, the candle was still there, and the matches worked, and the tunnel was no more scary than it had always been. Once inside the house, Robin ran. She ran through the big empty rooms, up the stairs, and down the hall to the door of the Velvet Room. She was back—and that made up for everything. It made up for everything the last few weeks had been: all the dirt, heat, discomfort, and all the hopeless ugliness and crowded confusion. It all seemed miles away in an instant.

Although she stayed most of the afternoon, she didn't do any reading that day. It was enough just to be there. She wandered around the room, letting her fingers drift along chair arms and table tops. She leaned her cheek against the cool beauty of the marble mantel. At the whatnot case she knelt down and pressed her nose against the glass in front of the portrait of Bonita. "Hi," she said. "I'm back."

The next day Robin went to work, but there wasn't much fruit. Late in the morning, to her surprise, Gwen came to the shed looking for her. She wasn't needed, so Mr. Criley let her go. Gwen had had a wonderful time, and she had a lot of souvenirs from the Islands that she wanted to show Robin. So they went up to Gwen's room and looked at the things and talked.

Robin had wondered if Gwen would be different when she got home, but she seemed to be just the same. She looked different because her blond hair was bleached even lighter by the sun, and her skin was a deep golden tan. But she hadn't changed in other ways. She was still as friendly and enthusiastic as ever. And she still said exactly what she was thinking, no matter what.

Today Gwen was enthusiastic about school starting. Robin was surprised. "I thought you didn't like school," she said. "And what about that boarding school back East you were going to?"

"Oh, I don't really like school," Gwen said. "But I

like to see all the kids, and there's always lots more things to do during the school year. I'm not going to that boarding school after all. At least not this year. I flunked their old test." Gwen wiggled her shoulders in her familiar shrug. "Mom was furious," she added cheerfully.

"Will you be going to Lincoln School in Santa Luisa then?" Robin asked.

"Sure," Gwen said. "That's where I've always gone." Her face lighted suddenly. "Hey, we'll be in the same room. You're going to be in seventh grade, aren't you?"

"I'm not sure," Robin said. "Dad says we'll all probably have to be tested before we're placed because we've missed so much school lately. I ought to be in seventh, though. I mean, that's the grade I'd have been in if we hadn't moved around so much."

"Oh, they'll put you in seventh," Gwen said. "I'll bet you could even be in eighth, if you wanted to. But don't though. It'll be fun being in the same room. We'll have Mrs. Jennings for English and history. Most of the kids like her. She makes you work hard, but she's not mean or anything."

"It sounds like fun," Robin said. She sighed. It really did sound like fun—going every day, and starting in September.

While Gwen and Robin were talking, Carmela came up to tell Gwen that Miss Andrews had come. Gwen looked startled. "Wow!" she said. "I forgot she was coming. I'm going to be awful. I haven't practiced for years."

Robin was going to leave, but Gwen didn't want her to. "Come on down and wait for me. It won't take long. Miss Andrews can't stand me for very long at a time. I'm her most terrible failure."

So Robin went downstairs with Gwen and listened

while Gwen took her lesson on the big grand piano. Gwen really was pretty bad, but of course she hadn't practiced while she was in Hawaii. When Miss Andrews finally stood up with a deep sigh, Gwen said, "Miss Andrews, I'd like you to meet my friend, Robin Williams. Robin can really play the piano, Miss Andrews."

Robin was surprised and shocked. She'd come right from the pitting shed, so her feet were bare and she was wearing one of her oldest dresses. Miss Andrews smiled politely, but Robin recognized the sharp curiosity behind the smile.

"How do you do, Robin," Miss Andrews said. "Won't you play something for me? I'd love to hear you."

"Come on, Robin," Gwen said. "Play that one you played for me. The long one."

Robin wanted desperately to refuse, but she couldn't think how to do it gracefully. So she went over to the piano. She hadn't noticed how bad her hands really looked until she saw them on the keyboard. The apricot juice had stained her nails, and her thumbs were crosshatched with dozens of tiny scars from the pitting knife. Watching her stained fingers on the white keys, she started out badly; but she had never played on a grand piano before, and the rich tone impressed her so that she forgot about her hands. She even forgot about Gwen and Miss Andrews. When she finished, she wasn't sure if she had played well or badly. The sounds had been exciting, but that was because of the wonderful piano.

She didn't want Miss Andrews to have to say something about her playing, so she jumped up quickly. "I have to go home now," she said. "It was nice meeting you. Good-by, Gwen." She rushed out feeling stupid and awkward.

She was almost to the barnyard, scuffing along with her head down, thinking of all the things she should have said and done when Gwen caught up with her. "Why did you run off like that?" Gwen asked. "Miss Andrews thought you were great."

"Great!" Robin laughed. "Gwen McCurdy, you're making that up. What did she really say?"

"She did say that. She really did. At least that's what she meant. What she said exactly was . . ." Gwen arranged her face in a primly judicial expression. "What she really said was, 'Of course, the child is badly in need of training, but I think there *is* a real talent there.' And when Miss Andrews says something like that, it means *great!*"

From then on Robin became a regular visitor at the McCurdys' house on Wednesdays, when Gwen had her piano lessons. When Miss Andrews wasn't in too much of a hurry, she had Robin play for her, too. Robin had heard that Miss Andrews was the best piano teacher in Santa Luisa and that she was very expensive; but she must have understood how things were, because she never asked Robin if she wanted to take lessons. Even when she spent as much as half an hour helping Robin, she only called it "listening to Robin play".

In between lessons, Gwen often asked Robin to come and help her practice. Really Robin didn't help much, but they played duets and took turns practicing. Gwen said it was more fun that way. She said practicing got pretty dull when there was no one there to listen and make comments. And Mrs. McCurdy was gone so much, to clubs and meetings, that there usually wasn't anyone there except Carmela, and she was busy. Once in a while, though, when they were practicing, Gwen's father came in to listen.

Don McCurdy was a big man with a slow, easy smile. His face was brown from the sun, and he wore riding clothes most of the time. To her surprise, Robin found that it didn't make her a bit nervous to have Mr. McCurdy in the room. She could go on practicing and giggling with Gwen, just as if he weren't there.

It took longer before Robin could feel at ease around Mrs. McCurdy. When she had first begun to visit Gwen at the McCurdy house, Mrs. McCurdy was always polite, but her small tight smile made Robin feel a little guilty without knowing why. Then one day that started changing. Robin was on her way up to Gwen's room when Mrs. McCurdy stopped her. "I've been hearing some nice things about you, Robin," she said.

"Oh?" Robin said, feeling her face getting hot. There never seemed to be any sensible answer when people said things like that to you.

"I was talking to Miss Andrews yesterday," Mrs. McCurdy went on. "She was telling me that you are very talented musically. Miss Andrews thinks your interest in music has encouraged Gwen to take her piano more seriously. In fact, she thinks Gwen has improved remarkably since you two have been working together." Mrs. McCurdy's smile was quite different from the one Robin had seen before.

Robin couldn't think of anything to say so she only smiled and nodded. After Mrs. McCurdy had gone on down the hall, Robin thought for a moment before she started slowly up the stairs. Halfway up she stopped and extended her arm. "I dub thee Sir Robin," she said regally. Then she skipped on up the stairs.

A few days after pitting season was over, the Williams family made a very important trip to town. First, they went to the Lincoln School where all the children, except Shirley, were tested to determine their grade placement. The test seemed pretty hard to Robin, particularly the arithmetic, but she thought she did fairly well. Mr. Maywood, the principal, said the results would be mailed to them in a few days.

Next, they went on downtown to go shopping. This was a very important shopping trip because everyone had pitting money to spend.

The children spent most of their money buying shoes and clothing for school, but Mama spent some of hers on things for the cabin. Then they all had a five-cent hamburger, and Mama treated everyone to a movie. That is, everyone except Robin and Dad. Dad didn't want to see the movie, so he and Robin went to the library instead.

There weren't many people in the library that night, so Robin and Dad had it almost to themselves. They had a good time. Dad found a book of poetry and showed Robin some poems he'd liked when he was her age. He had Robin hold the book, and he recited "Ozymandias" and "The Destruction of Sennacherib" in such a dramatic whisper that it made tingles go up the backs of Robin's legs. It seemed just like old times, back in Fresno. When the library closed, the movie still wasn't over, so they went for a walk around town. They talked about old times in Fresno and things they'd done there, and Robin told Dad more about Bridget and all about Gwen and the McCurdys.

"And if only they put me in seventh grade," Robin said, "Gwen and I will be in the same room in school."

"Robin," Dad said, "I don't think you ought to let this friendship with Gwen become too important to you. I'm glad that you and Gwen have had such good times together, and she sounds like a very nice girl; but—well, school will be starting soon and things may be different."

Robin took his hand and squeezed it. She knew exactly what he was going to say. "Don't worry, Dad," she said. "I'm not going to get my feelings hurt. You don't have to warn me. I've already thought about it. Anyway, I like Gwen, but there are other things more important to me. Lots more important."

They walked on together for a while, just enjoying the night and the peaceful sleepy streets. But then Dad sat down suddenly on a bus bench, and Robin saw that his face looked very white in the moonlight. "Let's just sit a minute and rest our feet," he said, but his smile didn't hide the awful tiredness in his face. Somewhere inside, Robin felt fear move like a cold, dark wind.

They sat quietly, side by side, on the bench. The night was warm, and amber with summer moonlight, but inside the warmth was gone. Robin thought suddenly of the Velvet Room and wished she were there.

The Eye of a Storm

On the saturday before school started Dad suggested that Robin ask Bridget to have dinner with them. Robin wasn't sure that Bridget would be able to walk so far. And maybe she wouldn't want to have dinner in the Village. But she ran over to ask her, anyway; and Bridget said she'd be delighted.

Robin had been thinking of making a short visit to the Velvet Room, but she decided to go home instead to help Mama get things ready. She had some ideas about fixing up the cabin.

The main room of the cabin looked a little better since Mama had spent her pitting money; but of course there was just so much you could do for a room that had to serve as front room, kitchen, dining room, and bedroom for half the family. Mama had made some bright cotton curtains; there was a patch of linoleum in the kitchen end of the room; and the cots had new Indian-blanket covers.

Robin got Mama to let her put the boys' cot in the

136

bedroom just for the evening. By padding up the other cot and letting the cover hang almost to the floor, she made it look almost like a studio couch. Then, with the chairs arranged around close, that end of the room was like a real living room.

The other children ate their dinner while Dad and Robin walked over to get Bridget. Robin was going to eat with the grownups because she was Bridget's special friend. When they reached the cottage, Robin took Dad around back, so he could meet Betty and the other animals before they went in. Sure enough, Damon and Pythias were curled up on their favorite bench. Robin was just waking them up when Bridget came to the back door.

Robin started to introduce Dad, but somehow it didn't seem right just to say Bridget. Dad was always particular about calling grownups *Mr.* and *Mrs.* She was stammering as Bridget came to the rescue. "Mrs. Gunther," she said, "Bridget Gunther, but I'd be happy to have you call me Bridget, just as Robin does."

"In that case," Dad said, "you'll have to call me Paul." He nodded toward Robin. "Anyway, we've heard too much about each other to stand on ceremony." Robin could see that they were going to get along fine.

The evening turned out better than Robin had hoped. Mama had made beef stew and corn bread and even an apricot pie. The pie was a little burned on one side where the oven still didn't heat right, but otherwise it was a fine dinner. Bridget seemed to be having a wonderful time. Everyone was so busy talking and laughing that Robin didn't have time to worry about the old bent silverware and the rummage-store plates.

After dinner they all sat around and talked. The others

liked Bridget, too. She didn't get a bit excited when Cary showed her his tarantula in a jar. Instead she was interested, and told Cary some things about tarantulas that he hadn't known before. Robin could see that Cary was impressed. Before long Shirley was leaning against Bridget's chair, and as a rule Shirley wouldn't go near a stranger, not on purpose, anyway. Bridget even got Rudy to talk by asking his advice about her water pump, which wasn't working quite right. Soon Rudy was telling her all about how a pump works.

But most of all, Dad and Bridget talked. Dad had always been interested in California's history, and it turned out that Bridget was, too. And Bridget asked a lot of questions about the work Dad was doing. She asked him about the kind of work he did in the mule barns and what his job had been like during apricot season. They talked about wildlife in California, too. That was really interesting to listen to. Dad knew a lot of animal stories, and so did Bridget.

It was almost dark when Robin walked Bridget back to her cottage. On the way they talked about the Williams family. Robin was surprised to find out how much Bridget knew about them.

She even said, "Cary is very much like you, Robin. He has a quick and rebellious mind. He won't settle for too ordinary an existence." Robin was astonished that Bridget should have figured that out so quickly. She'd just begun to figure it out herself, and she'd been living with Cary for eight years. Until just a few weeks ago, he'd seemed only like a nuisance.

They were almost at the cottage when Robin said, "Do you think my father looks tired? He does to me. He looked just like that before he got sick the last time."

Bridget didn't answer right away; and when she did, she seemed to be speaking carefully. "Your father is an intelligent and capable man, Robin. He really should be doing work that is better suited to his abilities."

"I know," Robin interrupted eagerly. "Even back in Fresno, when we still had the dairy, Dad used to say sometimes that he wasn't cut out to be a farmer. He wanted to study music and history and be a teacher or something like that. But his father died and then there was Mama and all the kids, so he never got to finish school. But I guess I've told you about all that." She sighed. "The last time he was sick the doctor said he shouldn't ever do heavy work again. But he has to, because it's the only kind he can get."

Bridget squeezed Robin's hand comfortingly. "Well, it probably would be better if he didn't have to lift bales of hay or tramp all day in the hot sun. But he's happy to have a steady job, and that will help to keep him well. Happiness always helps a lot."

Robin tried to tell herself that Bridget was right. Dad just couldn't get sick now when things were so much better. But there was a corner of fear at the back of her mind that she just couldn't get rid of.

The next Monday was the beginning of school. Robin was so excited that she felt a little bit sick. For the first time since third grade, she was starting school on the first day and really planning on being there all year.

Best of all, she was to be in seventh grade. The letter from the principal had said that although she was a little below grade in arithmetic she was very high in other subjects, so they had decided to let her try seventh. Rudy and Theda and Cary were all placed a year behind. Rudy was to be in the first year at Santa Luisa High, and Theda was in eighth grade. Cary, who had been to school only a few days at a time, would be in second. He was upset because he thought he should be in third, since he was eight years old. But Robin told him he'd done well to make second, considering how little he'd been to school.

That Monday morning as Robin stood waiting for the bus with all the other boys and girls from Las Palmeras, she couldn't tell whether she was scared or happy. Whichever it was, she didn't feel much like talking so she just listened to Gwen who was chattering away, just as she always did. At least part of Robin's mind was listening to Gwen; the other part kept dashing off in one direction after another. Would she like Mrs. Jennings? How did the other boys and girls at Lincoln School feel about kids from Las Palmeras Village? Would it be a good year or bad? It was so important. A school year lasted such a long time.

The first day of school turned out to be both good and bad, but mostly good. And it was the same way with the days and weeks that followed. There were good times and bad ones. Mrs. Jennings, who was her homeroom teacher, was one of the good things. It seemed to Robin that almost from the first day Mrs. Jennings took a special interest in her. Later she began to suspect that Mrs. Jennings made everyone feel that way. She had a way of calling people up to her desk for little private chats while the rest of the class worked on an assignment.

When Mrs. Jennings discovered how Robin felt about books, she gave her a list of good books to read. Some of the books Robin already knew, but she'd never even heard of some of them. It was Mrs. Jennings who taught Robin to read a book from the outside in, as well as from the inside out. Before that year Robin just jumped into every book she could get hold of and lived it. She had never thought of judging a book except by how it made her feel. If it made her feel good, she liked it; and if it made her feel bad or nothing much at all, she didn't. But that year Robin learned to let a part of her mind stand off and look at a book as she read. She learned that there were good writers, and writers who weren't so good; that some books were original, well written, and believable, and some were not. It seemed strange at first to criticize a book, because books had always seemed sacred; but it was exciting to learn to make a judgment on your own and back it up with reasons.

As far as school work went, it was a good year, the best Robin had ever had; but in other ways it was often a time of confusion and unhappiness. Sometimes it was like walking along the top of a wall with a bad fall waiting on either side.

She hadn't been at Lincoln School very long before she found out that it did make a difference whether or not you were one of the "Santa Luisa kids." In the seventh grade it was a quiet difference; no one called you names or refused to talk to you. In class and in the halls everyone was friendly. But at noontime, when everybody sat around in groups to eat lunch, all the kids who had grown up in Santa Luisa ate together. And the Village kids and others from farm labor families had their own groups. The Santa Luisa kids belonged to the school clubs and won all the elections; and for parties or anything outside of school the difference was even more important.

Because of Gwen, Robin was sort of in between. Gwen was important in the seventh grade at Lincoln School. And it wasn't just because she was a McCurdy. There were others, like Laura Greenfield, whose families were well-known, but who were not important the way

Gwen was. It was her bouncy good nature, her blond cute-
ness, and her cheerful impudence. Everybody liked Gwen
—and Gwen liked Robin. And that didn't change, even
when Gwen was back among all her old friends, as Robin
had thought it might.

Gwen wasn't the kind of person who paid attention
to the way things had always been done. If she wanted
Robin to eat with her gang, Robin did; and with a few ex-
ceptions, like Laura, no one seemed to mind.

Laura was the kind of girl who had always had everything, and didn't like any of it much. She was smart, but
her grades weren't very good. Robin thought it was be-

cause Laura used all her time and energy finding out people's tender spots. She was an absolute genius when it came to knowing just what a person couldn't stand to be teased about.

"Robin," Laura would say in a sticky voice, "where'd you get that cute dress. Isn't that the cutest dress? Don't you like Robin's dress? Where'd you get it Robin?"

So Robin would have to say that the dress came from the Dollar Store. There was no use lying about it, because one just like it was hanging in the window of the store. Then Laura would say: "Oh, really! Well, I'm going to have to tell my mother to shop for me at the Dollar Store. She always goes to the same old places like Olivia's or Beauchamp's." Then Laura and one or two others would giggle. But Laura had to be careful not to let Gwen notice what she was doing. Lots of times Gwen didn't notice. But when she did see what Laura was up to, she usually said something simple and right to the point, like, "Why don't you shut up, Laura?" And Laura did.

At home at Las Palmeras there were good times and bad, too. There were good times at the McCurdy's. At least twice a week Robin spent the afternoon there, studying with Gwen. Besides practicing the piano, she helped Gwen with her English and history assignments; and Gwen, who was best at arithmetic, made Robin really learn the multiplication tables for the first time in her life. Sometimes, when they were studying, Carmela would bring up some hot chocolate or Mrs. McCurdy would drop in to see how they were coming along.

When they were through studying, Robin would go home to the Village; but when winter came, it was dark by then, so Mr. McCurdy would walk part way with her or even drive her home in his car. Robin liked Mr. Mc-

Curdy and she could tell that he liked her. On the way to the Village they always found interesting things to talk about. That is, Robin did most of the talking, but Mr. McCurdy had a way of getting her started. Next to Dad, Robin had never met a grownup who was so easy to talk to.

Of course, there were good times at Bridget's, too. Robin still staked Betty out every day and got up early to have time for a little visit with Bridget. Several times, in the evening, Dad walked Robin over to the cottage for a visit and stayed to talk for a while. Bridget and Dad always had a lot to talk about. Dad said it was remarkable how much Bridget knew, considering how little she was able to get around. She took an interest in things that you wouldn't expect her to care about.

That winter, the bad times came when Gwen was busy with her family, or away on party invitations that, of course, did not include Robin. Then there were two whole weeks when Gwen was home with the flu. Without her, Robin didn't seem to belong anywhere. Laura and her friends made it plain that Robin didn't belong with the Santa Luisa gang; and the Village kids were just as bad when she tried to eat with them. Even Theresa, who had always been friendly, turned her back and said something about why didn't she go back to the "reech keeds." Sometimes, when she came home from school smarting from something Laura had said, or when someone from the Village called her "stuck up," it seemed as if everything was just in miserable confusion.

There were other bad times when from behind a book she watched Dad sitting at the table in the cabin. His head would sink low over his cup of coffee, and his freckles would stand out sharply against the paleness of his skin.

He would sit there as if he was just too tired to get up and go to bed. As Robin lay on her cot pretending to read, she would get angrier and angrier. She was angry at whatever it was that trapped people in jobs that weren't good for them. She was angry at the tiny, ugly cabin that didn't even have a decent chair for Dad to stretch out in, the way Mr. McCurdy stretched out in his big chair in front of the fireplace. She was even angry at Mama, who went on bustling cheerfully around without even noticing how tired-to-death Dad was getting.

But of course, there was a way to make everything all right. There was always something she could do whenever there was too much worry or confusion or anger. There was the Velvet Room. Once in a while Robin was able to visit it by sneaking away right after school. A few other times she managed to go in the evening right after dinner, but she couldn't stay long because it soon got dark. But it helped even when it wasn't possible to go there. Just knowing it was there made all the things that seemed to be pressing in on her move back. The Velvet Room was the center of everything all that fall and winter; a quiet core in the middle of confusion—like the eye in the center of a storm.

The Letter That Changed Everything

CHRISTMAS came and went. It was a good Christmas; at least it was much better than any the Williams family had had since they left Fresno. Bridget came to dinner on Christmas Day, and it was a real holiday meal. There was even a Christmas tree. Of course, it wasn't a very big tree, and the decorations were only popcorn and tinsel from cigarette packages; but it was a real tree, and there were presents under it.

During most of the two weeks' vacation, Gwen was busy with trips to Los Angeles and holiday parties; but Robin found plenty to do. She spent most of several days at Bridget's cottage. She was making some new dish towels for Mama, and Bridget was teaching her how to embroider them. In between cross-stitching and making French knots, she played with Bridget's animal family, and, of course, she made several visits to the Velvet Room. Except for one thing it was a very satisfactory vacation. And that one thing seemed to cancel out everything else.

Dad was worse. It was unmistakable. He looked paler and thinner than ever, and at times he seemed almost too tired to talk. Mama didn't notice, or at least she didn't seem to. She certainly didn't mention it, and all her plans were just as cheerful and hopeful as ever. But it was plain enough to Robin. She remembered how Dad had been just before he got so sick the last time. And there was something else she remembered, over and over and over. No matter how hard she tried not to think about it, it kept coming back to her—the words she had overheard the doctor say to Mama in the hall of the county hospital. "Your husband must not have pneumonia again, Mrs. Williams. He won't make it through another time." That was just exactly what the doctor had said.

But there was nothing Robin could do, nothing at all. There was nothing anyone could do. So most of the time she just tried hard not to think about it. When school began again and she had to get ready for semester examinations, there wasn't much time for either fun or worry, and she was almost glad.

There wasn't even time for the Velvet Room. She did regret this. And then early one Saturday morning, late in January, she was on her way home from Bridget's when she heard the thud of hoofs and Gwen's voice calling her name.

She answered and ran toward the sound. Gwen, on Mirlo, appeared around an orange tree. "Hi," Gwen said, "I was looking for you at your house, and your mother said you were at Bridget's. Here, give me your hand."

Robin put her foot in the stirrup; Gwen tugged; and in a moment they were galloping off through the orchard. "Where are we going?" Robin asked.

"To Palmeras House," Gwen said. "Mrs. Criley and

Carmela are going to clean it today. I thought you'd like to see it. You're always talking about it and everything. I asked Dad, and he said it would be all right if we went in and looked around while they're cleaning."

Robin was horrified. Would she be able to pretend well enough? How could she "ooh" and "ahh" over everything as if she hadn't seen it before? And besides, she didn't want to see Mrs. Criley and Carmela in her Velvet Room. She didn't even want to see Gwen there, really. It wasn't the kind of thing you could share with anyone.

"My mother didn't say I could go, did she?" Robin asked desperately. "She told me I had to hurry right home today to help with the washing."

"She said it was all right," Gwen said. Robin had forgotten that Gwen was able to talk Mama into anything. There just didn't seem to be any way out of it. There was nothing to do but pretend as best she could and hope that Gwen didn't notice anything.

When they reached Palmeras House, a truck was turning into the weed-grown drive. It stopped just opposite the entryway, and Mrs. Criley and Carmela got out. Then a terrible thing happened: Fred Criley got out of the driver's seat. He went around to the back of the truck and unloaded a lot of brooms and mops and a vacuum cleaner. Then he unlocked the big double front doors, and the three of them went in, with a clatter of mops and pails. Robin started after them in dismay. As if things weren't bad enough, to see Fred Criley in the Velvet Room would be just too awful.

Gwen had jumped down off Mirlo and was tying him to a railing. "Come on," she said. "What's the matter with you? You look funny."

"Nothing," Robin said, getting down off the horse.

"It's just that old Fred Criley. I don't like him."

Gwen nodded. "Me neither. He makes me sick." She shrugged. "Come on. He won't bother us. Let's go in."

Pretending wasn't as hard as Robin had thought it would be. Right at first, when they stepped into the wide entry hall with its upward sweeping staircase, Robin's, "Oh, isn't it beautiful!" sounded stiff with pretense; but then she started imagining that she really hadn't seen any of it before, and after that it was almost fun: like being an actress. She was sure Gwen didn't suspect a thing.

They went through the downstairs and the Spanish wing first. When they were in the room with the built-in bookcases, Gwen didn't say anything about the secret passage, so either she didn't know about it or she wasn't supposed to tell.

When they finally reached the Velvet Room, there was no one there but Carmela. She was down on her knees cleaning the woodwork, and when the girls walked in, she jumped as if she'd been stuck with a pin. "Oh!" she gasped. *Madre mía!* You frighten me."

Gwen smiled at Robin. "Carmela doesn't like it here very much," she whispered. "She's always worrying about *La Fantasma.*"

As Carmela went back to her polishing, Robin thought gratefully that it was a good thing she had been too busy to visit the Velvet Room lately. Carmela would really be nervous if the room had been freshly dusted when she arrived that morning. As Gwen showed Robin all around the room, she concentrated on keeping up her pretense of surprise. The beautiful old books, the huge leather inlaid desk, even the velvet-draped alcove, all the things with which she was so intimately familiar had to be commented on and admired. Even though Robin was very busy keeping her mind on saying just the right thing, something kept bothering her. Something seemed to be missing. She actually looked around several times to see what it might be before she realized that what she was missing wasn't anything she could see—it was a feeling. The room, with Gwen beside her and Carmela bustling around in the background, was only a beautiful room. The feeling was gone. The thing she'd been missing was the wonderful private promise of the Velvet Room.

It was a frightening thing to discover. If she went away as soon as possible, and then didn't come back for a few days, would all be the same again? She tried to steer Gwen toward the door, but there were still a few more things to see. They were still standing in front of the whatnot case when the door opened and Fred Criley walked in. He swaggered over and stood looking over their shoulders.

"What's all that stuff?" he demanded.

Gwen twisted her mouth in distaste. "Pictures and things," she said shortly.

"Them real jewels?" Fred asked, pointing to the small stones in the frames of the miniatures.

Gwen shrugged. "I guess so," she said. "Would you like to go now, Robin? We've seen just about everything."

"All right," Robin said, trying not to let her enormous relief show in her voice. "We might as well."

For weeks and weeks Robin had put herself to sleep at night by thinking about the Velvet Room, but that night she couldn't. The peace and comfort were gone. When she tried to picture it, Fred Criley's cocky face kept drifting into the scene. Finally, she just gave up and went to sleep feeling lost and lonely.

The next day, she knew she couldn't wait long to go

back. She had to go that day. And finally she found a
chance to slip away. She was almost afraid to go. On her
way there—in the orchard, through the tunnel, even in
Palmeras House itself—she felt tense and worried. What
if it wasn't the same? What if the magic was still missing?
But the moment she opened the door and stepped inside
the Velvet Room, she knew that everything was all right.

It looked the same, of course, only cleaner; but that
wasn't what was important. The important part was that
it felt the same, the same as ever. She closed the door
behind her, ran into the middle of the room, and spun
round and round until she landed in a heap on the floor,
dizzy and giggling. Whatever else happened, no matter
what else went wrong, there would always be the Velvet
Room.

But the very next day the letter came that changed
everything. Robin went to the mailbox herself. She noticed
that there was a letter from Uncle Joe, but she didn't feel
particularly curious about it, even though it wasn't like
Uncle Joe to write a letter.

Uncle Joe Spaulding was really Dad's uncle, and
though he was Dad's only relative, he had always seemed
like a stranger to Robin. Even when the Williamses had
seen him fairly often, before they left Fresno, he'd seemed
like a stranger. Uncle Joe was just that kind of man.

Robin remembered that when they had visited him at
his store, he would give each of the children one-half of
an apple. He never gave them a whole apple, and not
even a piece of candy from the counter near the cash register. Uncle Joe ran a shabby little grocery store and souvenir
shop a few miles outside Fresno, on the highway that led
to the mountain resorts. Out behind the store was a row
of motor cabins that hadn't been used for years and years.

Uncle Joe had closed them up when his wife died because he was too stingy to hire anyone to do the cleaning and make the beds. Spaulding's Grocery and Souvenirs didn't have any close neighbors, and Uncle Joe didn't have any friends. Robin thought he liked it that way. She had heard him say once that the reason he liked the tourist trade was that you seldom had to meet the same customer twice.

Robin didn't hear about what was in the letter from Uncle Joe until that night right after dinner. Mama was never very good at playacting, and there was something unnatural about her voice when she said, "Robin, I'm going out to get some wood now. You come along and help." Robin was puzzled. The woodbox was almost full, and besides, the boys usually got the wood.

Mama didn't look at Robin on the way to the woodpile; but when she started loading the wood on Robin's outstretched arms, she suddenly said, "Robin, we're going to have to move."

Robin almost dropped the stack of logs. "Move?" she cried. "When? Where?"

"I haven't time to tell you about it now. Dad's going to tell all of you soon, but I wanted to talk to you first. Dad's worried about moving for a lot of reasons, but because of *you* most of all." Mama had forgotten about loading wood, and Robin stood there with her heart feeling just as her arms did under the heavy pile of logs. "It'll be harder for you to leave than the rest of us—because of Bridget and Gwen and doing so well in school and all. But you're just going to have to pretend that you don't care much. This new job won't be nearly so hard for your Dad, and he's just *got* to take it!"

Robin was so surprised at the fierceness in Mama's

voice that for a moment she forgot the dreadfulness of what she had just heard. So Mama *had* known and worried about Dad all the time she had seemed so unnoticing. With a feeling of shock Robin wondered what else Mama had been hiding beneath her cheerful chatter.

When they came back into the cabin, Robin tried to look natural, but Dad glanced at them sharply as if he suspected something. He went back to his newspaper, however, and nothing more was said until Rudy and Theda had finished their homework. Robin had pretended to do hers, but her mind was in such a turmoil that she accomplished very little. Finally, Dad put down his paper and said. "Well, now, if you'll all put your books down, there's something I want to talk over with you. You, too, Cary. I think you're old enough to vote in this election."

Dad explained how it was. There had been a letter from Uncle Joe. It seemed his doctor had advised him to sell his store and spend most of his time resting. But Uncle Joe didn't want to do that, so he had written to Dad. If Dad would come and run the store, Uncle Joe would pay him sixty dollars a month and they could have one of the motor cabins to live in. Only one cabin though; because with Mama and the girls there to do the cleaning, he'd be opening the rest up for tourists again. Dad said that as far as he was concerned, there were some pretty good reasons for accepting Uncle Joe's offer and some other pretty good reasons for not accepting it. There wasn't much difference in the pay, and a weather-beaten motor cabin wouldn't be an improvement over the Village houses, except for a little more indoor plumbing. Accepting would mean, of course, a change of schools for everybody in the middle of the year, just when they'd all been counting on staying a whole term in the same school.

They'd all made friends they would hate losing; and the green Santa Luisa Valley was certainly prettier than the flat dry country around Uncle Joe's. However, the job at Uncle Joe's would be permanent. And there was one other advantage: working with a pitch fork and shovel and hay hook all day seemed to be getting a little harder all the time, and the job at the grocery wouldn't require lifting anything much heavier than a few cans of tomatoes.

Dad stopped talking and looked around at the silent, stricken faces of the family. "I've decided to leave it up to you," he said. "Tomorrow morning we'll take a vote. That gives you a night to sleep on it. And that's just what I'm getting ready to do."

After Dad left the room, everybody started talking at once; all except Robin, who, in the confusion, drifted out the door and into the orange grove. It was dark outside with only a thin rind of moon in the black sky. Robin usually wasn't too brave about darkness, but the need to get away was very strong.

A way into the orchard she stopped and just stood staring in the direction of Palmeras House. She wasn't really thinking at all.

First, there was Uncle Joe's. She could see it plainly—the shabby store building crouched beside a skinny sycamore tree, whose ravel of shadow offered the only shade in miles and miles of flat dry land. She could see details she hadn't even known she remembered: the saggy screen door with the wide metal doorpull that said Coca-Cola in bright enameled letters, making the paintless door look even dingier in comparison; the glass tanks on the gas pumps in front of the store that filled themselves with a gurgling rush of amber liquid when a crank was turned; the deserted stuccoed cabins out in back, like a row of oversized ovens under the hot valley sun, forever broiling the same batch of dust and spiders and rusty bedsprings.

Then, Uncle Joe's was gone; and there was Gwen, leaning down from Mirlo's back, holding out her hand; there was Mrs. Jennings' face with its encouraging smile; there was the big black piano in the McCurdys' living room and Miss Andrews smiling and beating time with her hand, as she did when the music was going well; there was Bridget and the stone cottage and finally—bigger and clearer than anything else—there was the Velvet Room.

But that picture faded away, too, although Robin tried to make it stay; and she could see Dad's face the way he had looked that night in Santa Luisa when he had sat down on the bench to rest—pale and thin and very tired.

On her way back to the cabin a little later, Robin met Mama, who was just coming back from the rest-room.

"Oh, there you are," Mama said. "I couldn't imagine where you'd gone to so quickly. One moment you were right there beside Cary, and a minute later you'd disappeared." But she didn't say anything about "wandering off"; and just before they got to the cabin, she put her arm around Robin's shoulders and gave her a quick squeeze.

"I was just out by the orchard," Robin said. "I was thinking." But it hadn't really been thinking. At least, not the kind of thinking that arranges things in an orderly fashion in your mind so that in the end you can see a pattern and meaning to things. It had only been a bewildering blur of memories and ideas and hopes and feelings. When Robin went to sleep that night, she still didn't know how she would vote.

Choices and Reasons

At breakfast the next morning Mama passed a coffee can around for everyone's vote. Up to the minute when the pencil was poised over the scrap of paper, Robin didn't know what she was going to do. But some hidden part of her mind must have been working on it secretly because, with the pencil in her hand, she didn't hesitate. She just wrote "go" as quickly as she possibly could and dropped her ballot in the can. Then she jumped up and ran out of the cabin, and no one tried to stop her and make her come back.

It was a hard day at school, and that afternoon she went straight to Palmeras House and up to the Velvet Room. In the alcove she pulled all the drapes shut so that it was almost dark, and she was alone in a soft reddish twilight. Then she collapsed on the window seat and began to cry. She hadn't cried for a long, long time, not since she was a very little girl back in Fresno. But that Tuesday afternoon she cried enough for all the times in between when she had wanted to and hadn't, for all the fear and shame and confusion of those three years, as well as for what she would lose when she left Las Palmeras. When at last the tears were gone, there wasn't anything left—except a strange empty numbness.

That afternoon was the end of crying. After that Robin was able to take part in conversations about notifying Lincoln School and in all the other preparations for leaving without tears or even a quaver in her voice. Even when Dad said, "I know how you feel, Robin, and I'm sorry," with so much sympathy in his voice, she was able to answer calmly.

"It's all right, Dad. I don't mind."

Strangely enough it was true. Nothing seemed to matter any more. It was almost as if all the feelings Robin had ever had were drained away by the tears that had soaked the cushion in the alcove of the Velvet Room. During the next few days she listened with a faraway calmness as Mrs. Jennings told her how sorry she was to see her go, and Miss Andrews urged her to try someday to go on with her music, and Gwen stormed around vowing that she wasn't going to let her go. Nothing broke the wall of calm, not even Bridget, when her dark eyes filled with tears and she said, "My dear, I'll miss you so much."

During the Williamses' last week at Las Palmeras the weather was clear and cold. Almost every night the smudge pots were fired in the orchards to protect the trees from the frost. Dad agreed to stay on until the cold snap broke, since he and Rudy were needed on the smudging crews. But as early as Thursday afternoon Robin began helping Mama pack for the trip to Fresno. The Williamses had collected a few new belongings during their stay at Las Palmeras, and it wasn't going to be easy to fit everything in and on and around the Model T.

Dad came in from the mule barns at about his usual time, but as he walked in the door, there was an unusual look about him. He hardly said hello before he added, "Robin, you go outside and stay until you're called. I want to talk to your mother."

From the front steps Robin could hear the murmur of their voices. She didn't feel really curious. After a while she stopped thinking about what they might be saying. She was remembering how she had hated their cabin when they first came because it was not what she had been hoping for. But then afterward she had come not to hate it any more because it was familiar and because of all the good things about living at Las Palmeras. Leaning forward, with her chin on her knees, she studied the hard-packed earth around the bottom stair. She could remember some other little patches of earth that she had known well. It was funny how well acquainted you could become with a certain arrangement of clods and stone and twigs and ant holes. As she pondered, Dad came out carrying her sweater. "Come on, Robin," he said. "I want you to go up to the McCurdys' house with me."

It wasn't a long walk to the big house, but that day Dad took the Model T. The old car made such a racket on the rough dirt road that it wasn't worthwhile even trying to talk; but when it had jangled to a stop near the McCurdys' house, Dad said, "Robin, the McCurdy's have something very important to ask you. I'll let them tell you about it; but I just want to let you know that your mother and I have discussed it, and we're going to leave it up to you. I'm not happy about making you accept the responsibility for such a big decision; but for reasons you'll understand when you have children of your own, I feel I haven't the right to decide for you. Just remember that however you decide, I'll understand."

Robin got out of the car reluctantly. Somehow the word "decision" made her feel frightened. Dad smiled reassuringly as he leaned over and closed the door. The Model T groaned into reverse, backed and turned loose-jointedly, and clattered away toward the Village, leaving Robin standing all alone outside the McCurdys' house. As if in a trance, she started up the walk.

The door flew open before she could reach it, and Gwen bounced out looking happy and excited. She grabbed Robin's hand and pulled her down the hall toward Mr. McCurdy's study. "Come on," she said. "Hurry! Mom and Dad want to talk to you."

In the study Mrs. McCurdy was standing near the window. Mr. McCurdy patted the leather couch beside where he was sitting. "Come in and sit down, Robin," he said. "And you run along, Gwen. You can talk to Robin later."

"Oh, let me stay," Gwen begged. "I'll be quiet. I'll let Robin decide. I won't say a word."

Mrs. McCurdy laughed. "You wouldn't have to say anything, dear. There's at least a volume written all over your face. Now run along."

Gwen backed out the door, still protesting. When her excited face finally disappeared, Mrs. McCurdy came over to the fireplace. She leaned against the mantel and smiled her special smile at Robin. Standing there, against the dark wood of the mantel, she looked like a painting; but to make the picture complete, she ought to have been holding a little pug-faced dog or a frilly fan.

No one said anything for a minute, and Robin was beginning to feel very uncomfortable. She looked down at her hands folded neatly in her lap. Then Mr. and Mrs. Mc-Curdy both started talking at once. "Robin," they said. They both laughed, and Robin managed a weak smile. "Let me explain it, Don," Mrs. McCurdy said.

"Robin," she said, "we've been discussing with your father the possibility of your staying here with us at Las Palmeras until the end of the school year. As you might guess, it was Gwen's idea at first; but Mr. McCurdy and I agree that it would be a fine arrangement. Gwen is so fond of you, and she insists that nothing in the world would make her happier." She paused and smiled again.

Robin opened her mouth, but for a moment nothing came out. "What did Dad say?" she managed at last. "Did my dad say I could stay?"

"Yes, he did," Mr. McCurdy said. "We pointed out to your dad that he would be doing us a big favor by letting us borrow you for a while this way. Gwen is lonely here. The ranch takes such a lot of my time, and Mrs. McCurdy's clubs and things keep her pretty busy. And Gwen's certainly been doing better work at school and on her music since you two got together. When we put it that way, your dad said he'd leave it up to you. He said he'd be willing to abide by your decision."

"Your father agreed that it would be a shame for you to have to change schools in mid-term when you've been doing so well at Lincoln," Mrs. McCurdy added. "And it seems to mean a lot to him that you could continue with your piano here. I know Miss Andrews will be pleased to have you as a regular pupil. She is *so* enthusiastic about your musical ability."

Robin stood up suddenly. So many things were whirling through her mind that they kept getting all mixed up. She started backing toward the door. "I . . . I don't know."

To her relief Mr. McCurdy interrupted. "How would it be if you let us know tomorrow? This is a pretty important decision for you to make. Maybe you'd like to think about it and talk it over with your family."

"Yes," Robin said quickly. "I would. I'd like to think it over." She turned and hurried from the room. Just outside the door she stopped and rushed back. "Thank you," she said. "Thank you for . . ." She made a helpless little gesture and rushed away again.

Gwen was waiting in the kitchen. She threw her arms around Robin and bounced her up and down. "Isn't it wonderful!" she squealed. "Isn't it great?" They walked as far as the stables together, with Gwen chattering enthusiastically all the way. She had all sorts of plans. Robin was to have the blue room, right next to hers. They were going to be like real sisters and do everything together. Mr. McCurdy had promised to bring a cow pony down from El Pasto so they could ride together, and it would be just like Robin's own horse as long as she stayed at Las Palmeras. Of course, when summer came, Robin would have to go back to her folks; but next year when school started again —well, Gwen hadn't mentioned it to anyone yet, but she would after a while, and she was sure Robin could come back then, too.

Robin agreed that it was wonderful and that she was excited but she didn't have to say much because Gwen was so busy talking. When they reached the stables, Gwen turned back and Robin began to run, past the stables, past the barns, past the Criley's house, until finally she had to stop and catch her breath at the hedge of eucalyptus trees. Then she went on more slowly. When she reached the Williamses' cabin, she climbed the stairs very quietly and stopped at the door. She just stood there for a while on the top step because somehow she couldn't go in, not just yet.

But the minutes passed, and nothing happened. She still couldn't seem to think very logically. For one thing, the sun had gone down over the tops of the hills, and it was suddenly very cold. Nobody could make an important decision while she shivered all over and her teeth chattered up and down. And besides, she kept hearing things from inside the cabin.

Through the thin door she could hear the murmur of voices, Theda's mostly, and Mama's. She heard Dad cough and the funny noises Cary always made when he was pretending to be some kind of a machine. Then quite clearly she heard Shirley calling from the bedroom. Her voice had a fuzzy, sleepy sound. "Robin, I need Robin to read me to sleep."

Without even knowing she meant to, Robin turned and tiptoed down the stairs. She began to run again, this time into the orchard. The aisles between the trees were lined with smudge pots so that she had to keep dodging around them as she ran. But she didn't slow down until she was almost at Bridget's cottage.

It was a strange time for a visit, but Bridget didn't seem very surprised. At least she didn't ask any questions until she had hurried Robin in and sat her in front of the fire, then she put some milk on the stove to heat. When they were both sitting in front of the fireplace with steaming mugs of hot chocolate, Bridget asked, "Did you want to tell me something?"

"Yes," Robin said. "I have to decide something and . . . well, I guess I've already decided, really, but I want to

talk about it to someone. If I told you about it, would you tell me what you think?"

"Of course, dear. I'd be glad to tell you what I think, if you feel it would help."

It was hard to find a starting place. Bridget knew part of the story, but Robin wanted to start at the very beginning because it was so important to make her understand. It all seemed to start a long way back. There was the letter from Uncle Joe and Bridget had to understand what it was like at Uncle Joe's store in the San Joaquin Valley. There was having to move again, and start all over at a new school. There was never seeing Gwen again, or Bridget. There was losing the grand piano and the lessons from Miss Andrews. And then all of a sudden there was the chance to stay—the chance to stay at Las Palmeras.

"So I have to decide what to do," Robin said. "In a way it all seems wonderful, like a dream come true. But there's my family, Dad and Shirley and Cary and everybody. I don't know what it would be like—seeing them go without me."

"But you said at first that you'd already decided," Bridget said. "What is it that you've decided to do?"

Robin turned away from Bridget's dark eyes. "I'm going to stay here, with the McCurdys," she said; and there was a defiant ring to the words that she hadn't known would be there. Bridget said nothing at all, and after a while Robin asked, "Do you think that's a bad decision? You do, don't you?"

"No, Robin," Bridget said softly. "Not necessarily. It may be a good decision. It depends, I think, on your reasons for deciding. Many of the things we do are not right or wrong in themselves. But our reasons for doing them can be very right or very wrong. Have you thought about your reasons for wanting to stay with the McCurdys?"

"I told you," Robin said quickly. "I was just telling you all the reasons. Aren't they good ones?"

"Yes, they are," Bridget said. "Wanting to continue your music and to go to a fine school like Lincoln are very good reasons. If they are real ones. And wanting to be with Gwen is fine, too, if it is really very important to you."

Robin's head dropped again. "I like Gwen," she said. "She's the best friend I ever had. I like her a lot."

"Of course you do," Bridget said, "and I know you like her parents, too. But somehow I don't think the Mc-Curdys are really your reason for wanting to stay at Las Palmeras."

There was a scratching at the door, and Bridget went to let in Damon and Pythias and give them a bowl of bread and milk. While she was busy, Robin got up and went to the front window of the cottage. Through the winter-thinned grove of trees she could see part of the roof of Palmeras House. After a while Bridget came and stood beside her.

"Is that the real reason?" Bridget asked. "Has it something to do with Palmeras House?"

"No!" Robin said quickly. She whirled away and went back to her chair by the fire. Bridget followed more slowly. They sat side by side watching the flames leap, orange and gold against the blackened stones of the hearth. At last Robin took a deep breath. "Yes," she said. "Yes, I guess it is."

It wasn't easy to talk about the Velvet Room. There just weren't any words to explain what it had come to mean to her in the last few months. But somehow, as she tried, Bridget seemed to understand. "It makes everything different," Robin finished. "As if I was someone else, instead of me. Somebody wonderful and beautiful, that nothing bad could ever happen to."

"Someone like Bonita McCurdy?" Bridget asked with a teasing little smile.

"Yes," Robin said almost angrily. She wouldn't have told Bridget about pretending to be Bonita if she'd known that Bridget would laugh at her. "Yes," she repeated, this time intending the defiant tone, "someone like that, I guess."

The teasing smile was gone, and Bridget said gently, "But perhaps Bonita wasn't like that, Robin. Why would you want to be like Bonita when everyone believes something terrible happened to her? You know that some people even thought she was murdered."

"Well, I don't think so," Robin said. "I think she just went away—to get married or to be an actress or something. I don't think it was anything bad."

Bridget only shook her head slowly with a soft, sad smile. She sat looking into the fire, her quiet face showing no sign of what she was thinking. At last she said, "Last summer when I gave you the key to Palmeras House, I wondered if I'd done the right thing. But the house seemed to fascinate you so, and it was plain how much you were in need of something—beauty, perhaps. I thought it would help you . . ."

"Oh, it did," Robin interrupted eagerly. "It's helped me more than anything in my whole life."

"Yes," Bridget agreed, "I think it has helped. But you mustn't let it be too important. You mustn't let it take the place of more important things. You can't stop counting on people, Robin."

Robin turned her face away as something welled up inside her—a dark wave of fear and resentment. "You have to," she said. "You have to stop counting on them. They can't help you, and you can't help them. There's no way to help at all." She jumped up and ran out of the cottage, down the path, and out the gate.

She took a few steps into the orchard before she came to an abrupt halt. For just a minute she stood there, frozen in her tracks like someone playing "statues," and then she began to run again. But her direction had changed. Now she ran not toward the Village, but back toward Palmeras House and the Velvet Room.

She ran fast because it was late and she'd have to be home soon, but that wasn't the only reason. She was running to get away from something, too. Something she'd caught a glimpse of in Bridget's cottage.

The tunnel was the same as always, blacker than any midnight, but there was a difference once she was inside the house. She'd never been there quite so late in the evening before. The huge old rooms were almost as dark as the tunnel itself. She would have to use the candle all the way to the Velvet Room.

She couldn't hurry because the air currents made the flames waver dangerously, and every room seemed endless as the walls faded back and back before the candle's tiny, unsteady light. But at last she was there. She stepped into the old familiar comfort and, just as she hoped it would, the door closing behind her shut out entirely whatever it had been that had made her run away.

She moved peacefully around the room, touching each familiar object, straightening a book on a shelf, and rearranging a lamp on a table. Her fingers drifted along the back of the red couch, and she bent to peer at the row of miniatures in the glass case. The jewels in the tiny frames twinkled charmingly in the candlelight. In the alcove she curled up on the velvet cushions and looked out at the darkness.

It would be lighter soon. The air was very clear and still, and a round moon was just coming up over the edge of the hills. In the magic of the moonlight it was easy to turn the dead weeds of the lawn to rich smooth green and to spread the curving drive with fresh white gravel. There might even be lanterns or torches lining the drive and slanting rectangles of light spilling out of all the tall windows. A carriage might pull up, drawn by high-stepping horses. It would stop right there, before the arched entry, and someone would get out. A young girl, perhaps, with dark hair piled high on her head and a long dress that shimmered in the torchlight.

Robin's imagining was interrupted suddenly by the realization that she was very, very cold. The moon was clear of the hills now and rising fast in the still, cold sky. She would have to hurry or they would be wondering where she was.

It was a cold walk home, and where the big trees shut out the moon it was very dark. But Robin didn't mind the cold, and the dark didn't seem frightening. It was as though nothing could touch her, now that she knew—really knew—what she was going to do.

She was sure now. There, in the tower, without thinking or planning or worrying at all, she had suddenly known that she could not leave.

Bridget's Story

WHEN ROBIN got home from Palmeras House that night, no one asked her where she had been. Perhaps they just supposed that she had been with Gwen all that time, talking and planning.

Cary and Shirley were already asleep, but the rest of the family was sitting around the wood stove when she came in. They all looked up quickly, and for a moment there was an uncomfortable silence. Dad took his feet down off an apple crate. "Come here and sit down, Robin," he said. "You look a little blue around the gills. Judging by your complexion, I'd say that Rudy and I will probably be out lighting smudge pots again before morning."

Rudy nodded and grinned. He tipped his chair back until he could reach his cot, where Cary was already curled up asleep, and pulled off a blanket. Then he leaned over and tucked the blanket around Robin's shoulders.

"Well?" Theda said suddenly, and there was an angry

sound to the word. "Are you going to stay with them?"

Robin could feel their eyes on her but she didn't look up. "Yes, I guess so," she said. "I guess I'll stay."

No one said anything at first, but Robin heard Mama catch her breath in a sharp little gasp. After a moment Dad stood up and put his hand on Robin's bowed head. "Well, there's no use denying we'll miss you, Robin," he said. "But it's the sensible thing to do. It will be a fine thing for you, and for Gwen, too. Come on now, everyone. Let's get to bed. If that thermometer keeps on dropping, Rudy and I won't get much sleep tonight."

Theda didn't say a word to Robin as they got ready for bed, and she didn't even give Robin her choice of curling up or stretching out, as she usually did. She just lay down with her back to Robin and her face to the wall. When Robin couldn't help touching her as she got into bed, she jerked away angrily. Robin lay there, miserable, clinging to her side of the cot to keep from rolling against Theda. She was cold and uncomfortable, and it took her a long time to get to sleep.

Sometime in the night she was awakened by a truck's horn, and a moment later someone banged on the door of the cabin. She heard Rudy groping around for the light cord in the center of the room, and she squeezed her eyes shut against the sudden glare of the naked bulb. When Dad came out of the other room, Rudy was sitting sleepily on the edge of his cot, putting on his shoes. The fire had gone out in the wood stove, and it was so cold in the cabin that Dad's breath made a fog as he bent over to whisper to Rudy. Robin knew they wouldn't be back until after sunup, tired, and sleepy and so black with oil smoke that they would look like actors in blackface makeup.

After Dad and Rudy had gone out and Mr. Criley's

truck had rumbled away into the cold night, Theda poked Robin with her toe. "Hey," she said, "are you awake?"

"Yes," Robin whispered.

"I just wanted to tell you I'm not mad anymore. I've been thinking about it, and I guess I understand. I guess I'd have done the same thing if it had been me."

"Would you?"

"Sure. If I had a chance to live in a house like that with a room of my own and everything I'd have said yes, too. Just think, the McCurdys will probably get you some new clothes, too. Things like Gwen wears. Or at least you'll get some of her old ones. It's a good thing she's taller than you are. Gee, I'll bet you get that terrific blue skirt she wears. You know, the plaid one with all the pleats. It's almost too short for her now. And maybe you'll even get that real woolly coat."

Theda went on chattering cheerfully about clothes and parties and what good times Robin was going to have, and Robin turned over and went back to sleep. Theda thought she understood, but she didn't really. She didn't understand at all.

The next day after school Robin went home with Gwen and stayed for dinner. It was the first time she had eaten dinner at the big house. Sitting at the huge table with just Gwen and her parents, with Carmela waiting on the table, was very different from the way things were at home. But everyone was very nice; and when Mr. McCurdy started talking about roundups at El Pasto, it was so interesting that Robin forgot to feel strange.

After dinner she went home to the cabin. As she came up the stairs, she heard someone talking to Mama, and there was Bridget sitting in a chair by the stove with a basket in her lap. Robin was surprised, because Bridget seldom went far from the cottage by herself. She was also a little embarrassed because of the way she had run away last night.

But Bridget's smile was the same as always, full of warmth and welcome. "Hello, Robin," she said. "I just had to come over to tell your mother good-by."

Shirley came over and leaned against Robin and wrapped her thin little arms around Robin's waist. "Mrs. Bridget brought us some jam," she said. "Strawberry jam."

Bridget picked up her cane and her basket. "I must be going now," she said. "Robin, do you suppose you could walk home with me? I'm a bit tired, and it's a great help to have someone's arm to hold over the rough ground in the orchard."

It was almost dark as Robin and Bridget picked their way over the furrows and around the smudge pots toward the stone cottage. Robin had a feeling that Bridget wanted to say something about last night, but she didn't seem to want to bring it up right away. Instead she kept talking about the weather and things like that. "Well, it doesn't look as if there'll be any smudging tonight," she said. "Not with this overcast coming in. And my, isn't it turning warm? It almost feels like spring is here."

It wasn't until they had reached the cottage and Robin had helped start the fire in the fireplace that she found out what Bridget really had in mind. "There's something I want to tell you, Robin," she said. "Sit down by the fire while I put some milk on to heat. I won't be a minute."

When Bridget came back to her rocking chair, she shut her eyes a moment. "Let me see," she said. "Where to begin? It's such a long story." Robin stared at her in bewilderment. Then Bridget smiled and leaned forward. "The diary. Perhaps you noticed when you were reading

Bonita's diary, that at times she signed herself *B.B.*?"

"Yes. I thought it was her nickname or something."

"It was," Bridget said. "It was a nickname her grandfather gave her because of her initials." She paused and then went on slowly and significantly. "You see, Bonita's full name was Bonita Bridget McCurdy."

Robin gasped.

Bridget nodded. "For many, many years my name has been Bridget Gunther, but when I was your age it was Bonita. Bonita Bridget McCurdy."

Robin could only stare in amazement. Bridget! Her own sweet ordinary Bridget was Bonita, the mysterious missing heiress of Las Palmeras.

"But it's a secret," Bridget went on. "It's a secret I've kept for many years, and I want you to promise that you'll not give it away."

"You mean nobody knows?" Robin finally managed to ask. "Not even Gwen or Mr. McCurdy?"

"No, the McCurdys don't know, and I don't want them to. You and I are the only ones who know."

"But what happened to Bonita—I mean, what happened to you? Where did you go when you disappeared and everyone thought you were dead?"

"Well, since you read the diary, I'll begin where it ended. After my grandfather died, the only family I had left were Aunt Lily and Uncle Francisco and their baby boy. And when my grandfather's will was read, I lost them, too. At least that's how it seemed to me. You see, when the will was read, it turned out that Grandfather had left all of Las Palmeras to me. Everyone was surprised—certainly I was. I'd known that Grandpa had thought of Francisco as a city boy with no interest in the land, but it had never occurred to me that he intended to leave the ranch to me. Of course he did leave a large sum of money to Francisco, but not an acre of Las Palmeras.

"I thought at first that it wouldn't make any difference, that we could all go on living at Las Palmeras as one family. But I soon found out different. Aunt Lily, particularly, was very unhappy. I suppose when she gave up her lovely home in the city, she pictured herself as the mistress of Las Palmeras, and naturally she was disappointed. And then the feud between Aunt Lily and María, my old nurse, became worse and worse. It made me very unhappy. Aunt Lily said that María was spying on her and demanded that she be sent away. And María kept hinting to me that Aunt Lily and Uncle Francisco were plotting against me—even that they meant to harm me.

"And then one night I had been reading in the library—" Bridget stopped and smiled, "the Velvet Room, that is—by the way, it was always one of my favorite places, too—and I fell asleep in the alcove with the curtains drawn. When I awoke, Aunt Lily and Uncle Francisco were in the library having a violent argument. I was afraid to come out for fear they might think I had been listening intentionally. I don't remember all of what they said, but it concerned the mistake they had made in selling Uncle Francisco's practice and their home in the city and in coming to Las Palmeras. Each was accusing the other of being responsible. But then Aunt Lily started talking about me. It seemed she believed, or at least she did for the sake of that particular argument, that I had schemed and plotted to get Grandfather to leave everything to me. Finally Aunt Lily ran from the room, and Uncle Francisco followed her.

"That same night I ran away. If I'd waited one day, I'm sure I would have found a better way to solve the problem. But I was not quite sixteen and was emotional and impulsive. I worried and cried half the night, until I was in such a state that I wasn't thinking very clearly at all. Part of the time I was grieving because it seemed to be my fault that Uncle Frank and Aunt Lily were so unhappy; and the rest of the time I was almost ready to believe that María was right when she said they were plotting to do away with me. It sounds pretty silly now, doesn't it? But in the middle of that lonely night, I wasn't sure. Anyway, I ran away. I didn't take anything with me except a little money and a few keepsakes because I was in such a hurry. One thing I did take, though, was the key to the tunnel passage. I guess I thought I might change my mind and want to come back and would need a way to get into the house."

"Oh," Robin said. "I wondered about that."

"Yes, I remember you asked about it. You see, I was not being untruthful when I said that Mr. McCurdy gave it to me. But it was my grandfather, the first Mr. Mc-Curdy."

There was a sizzling noise from the stove and the smell of burned milk. "Heavens!" Bridget cried. "The milk's boiling over. I forgot all about it."

Robin ran to the stove, put the steaming pan in the sink, and hurried back. "Let's never mind the cocoa right now," she said. "Why did people think you'd been murdered?"

"Oh, not many did. In fact, the police finally assumed that I had drowned. We'd had a very wet winter that year, and the river was in flood at the time. It was María who started the rumors. After I ran away, she went around hinting darkly that I'd been murdered. The authorities must have known that she had no reason to think so, but there were people who believed her. I guess it was years and years before some of the people of Santa Luisa were really friendly to my aunt and uncle. And of course you can still hear the ghost story."

"But Gwen said they looked everywhere for Bon—I mean, for you. She said the police looked and looked. Why didn't they find you?"

"They probably would have if I hadn't had help. Do you remember reading in the diary about my friend, Mary Ortega?"

"Yes, the one who was planning an elopement for the foreman's daughter."

"Yes," Bridget smiled. "Mary was always involved in some romantic adventure or other. And if none was handy, she was always able to manufacture one. I'm sure the week she hid me in her house was one of the happiest times of her life. That first night, when I ran away, I rode my little mare straight to the Ortegas' house. Mary and I had a secret entrance to her room that we had used when we were little girls—up a tree and over the veranda roof to her window. So I was able to get to Mary without anyone's seeing me. I told her everything, and of course she was sure that María was right and my life was in danger. Mary could make a trip to the dressmaker into a hairbreadth adventure, so you can imagine what she could do with my predicament.

"Anyway, she hid me in a little, unused attic bedroom and we just turned Conchita loose, knowing that she would find her way home. There was a shortcut between the Ortegas' ranch and ours that I never took in the rainy season, because it involved fording a creek. But Conchita was never timid about water, and she must have gone home by way of the ford, because when they found her outside the corral the next morning, her saddle and blanket were still wet. It had been an especially wet winter, and the

Santa Luisa River was in flood. A bridge had been partly washed away just a mile below here, a day or two before. So the police developed the theory that I had gone for an early morning ride, as I often did, and had forgotten about the bridge.

"It was a good theory, only Tomás and María and some of the others knew that Conchita would never have carried me onto a faulty bridge. And even if she had, and we had fallen, they knew I was too experienced a horsewoman to drown while my horse swam to safety. But I suppose that the police never asked Tomás and María for their opinions, so after a little while the authorities announced that Bonita McCurdy had died by drowning and that her body had been carried out to sea."

"But how did you get out of that attic?" Robin asked.

"Well, for a while it looked as if I just wasn't going to. I had to stay in that little attic room for almost a week, mostly because Mary was having such a good time sneaking food up to me and taking all sorts of unnecessary, elaborate precautions. I'm sure I would have reconsidered and gone home if it hadn't been for Mary's enthusiasm for the whole escapade. But Mary's aunt had written from San Francisco asking her to come for a visit, and Mary had decided that I should go to San Francisco, too, and look for a job as a governess."

"Is that where you went?" Robin asked. She had completely forgotten her own problems and was listening breathlessly. She had never heard such an exciting story in her whole life.

"Yes, indeed. And I'm sure our trip there was the masterpiece of Mary's lifetime. Someday I'll try to tell you about it. It's all a bit jumbled in my mind now, but as I recall it was an absolute maze of disguises, intrigues, and secret meeting places. But be that as it may, I did reach San Francisco and Mary found me a perfect job, with the family of a German professor in Berkeley. The Bauers were just over from Germany and they knew little English and less about American customs, so it didn't occur to them to investigate my background very carefully."

"And didn't Mary ever tell anyone where you were?"

"No, she never told. After a year or two, she did write, urging me to come home, but by then I was reluctant. And poor Mary didn't live to be very old. While I was still at Berkeley, she died of typhoid fever. And as far as I know she had never told anyone what she knew about my disappearance."

"And what did you do then?"

"I lived with Professor Bauer's family for four years. They were wonderful people. I was supposed to be teaching the children English, but after a while I was really a member of the family. The professor was very like my grandfather in some ways, and the oldest girl, Helga, was almost my age, and we became close friends. I was very happy there. Then when I was nineteen a young artist came to visit the Bauers. His name was Eric Gunther, and he was from Switzerland."

Bridget was silent for a moment, and her dark eyes were soft and cloudy. She seemed to be drifting away into old happy memories. "Gunther?" Robin prompted eagerly.

"That's right," Bridget said smilingly. "Eric and I fell in love and were married, and I went back to Switzerland with him."

"Didn't you ever tell him about Bonita McCurdy and Las Palmeras and everything?"

"Not for a long time. You see, Eric was a very independent person, and he never had a great deal of money of his own. Somehow it never was just the right time to tell him that I could claim a large inheritance if I wanted to. We were happy, and it seemed foolish to risk changing things. I always intended to tell him some day, but I kept putting it off—until just before he died. When he was very sick and we knew he hadn't long to live, I told him, because he was worried about leaving me with so little money. He made me promise to come back to Las Palmeras. That was about fourteen years ago. So, after he was gone, I came back to Santa Luisa. I had heard that my aunt and uncle had died some time before, I went to see a lawyer, and he told me how to go about proving who I was. But then I heard that Don McCurdy and his new wife were looking for a housekeeper, and I decided to apply, just to look the situation over and to see Donie again. I'd always remembered what a sweet baby he had been."

"Didn't anyone recognize you?" Robin broke in.

"No, thirty-three years is a long time. And, of course Mr. McCurdy was just a baby when I left Las Palmeras. No, no one knew who I was. So then I just took the job as housekeeper and told the lawyer that I'd decided not to let anyone know after all. And in a little while Gwen was born and I became her nurse."

"What made you decide not to tell that you were Bonita?" Robin asked.

Bridget didn't answer right away. For a time she only sat staring into the fire. "I don't know," she said finally. "I don't know, really. In a way you might say that I ran away again. Do you understand what I mean by that?"

It was Robin's turn to ponder. After a while she said, "I guess I don't understand, not really. Because you didn't really run away again, did you?" Bridget shook her head. "Then I guess I don't understand, unless you mean you just did what was easiest for you at the time. Is that it?"

"That's it exactly. It was wonderful to be living at Las
Palmeras again, but somehow after all those years it was
easier not to have so much responsibility. And besides, I
liked Don and Catherine, and I didn't want to risk turning them into another Frank and Lily."

"Oh," Robin said suddenly, "there's something I've
been wanting to ask you about—the tunnel. Why is there
a tunnel?"

"Oh, yes, the tunnel. I should have explained that
to you before. It has quite a history. At the time the adobe
portion of the house was built, way back before my grandfather came to Las Palmeras, there had been unsettled
times in Southern California. There had been a bit of fight-
ing among the Spanish Californians over who was to be
governor of the state. And while the leaders of the state
were busy chasing each other around, there was no one to
interfere with the activities of gangs of bandits and rene-
gade Indians. So when the house was built, my great
grandfather, Francisco Montoya, had the tunnel made as
a way to escape in case the house was ever attacked."

"Was it ever attacked?"

"No, it never was. In fact, I remember my grandfather
saying that when he first came to Las Palmeras, the tunnel
was being used as a wine cellar. Anyway, as I told you, the
key was one of the few things I took away with me when
I ran away. Then, after I came back and Don and Catherine built the new house, I used the tunnel to visit the old
place now and then when I felt homesick. But in recent
years I've not been able to manage the ladder."

They sat silently for a while in front of the fire. Robin
was thinking that it was no wonder she had felt so close
to Bonita. She really had known her, all the time. As she

looked at Bridget's face, with its wide dark eyes and small
pointed chin, she could see why the miniature portrait had
looked slightly familiar.

It was a wonderful story, more fascinating than any
fairy tale. It was the best secret she had ever known, and
the most exciting. But then, like sticking a balloon with a
pin, Bridget thrust a question into Robin's excitement,
exploding it and leaving in its place only fear and a stubborn deafness.

"Do you understand, Robin, why I thought I must
tell you all this?"

Robin's eyes were on her fingers, which were carefully
folded and unfolding a pleat in her skirt. If she said yes,
perhaps Bridget wouldn't say anymore. "Yes," she said.
"I think so."

But Bridget didn't stop. "Do you see what my story
has to do with you, and with what you've decided to do?"
Robin nodded hastily, keeping her eyes down and her mind
closed; but she couldn't help hearing. "When I was Bonita
McCurdy, I had the Velvet Room, in fact all of Las
Palmeras, but it didn't help me. I had to leave it all behind
to find what was really important. Belonging to a place isn't
nearly as necessary as belonging to people you love and who
love and need you. I've lived a long time, Robin, but I
have never been happier than I was the years Eric and I
spent wandering all over Europe like gypsies—and we didn't
even have a Model T to call home."

Robin's face burned with resentment. Bridget had no
right to mention the Model T. It was like mentioning
someone's crossed eyes or crippled legs. But she only shook
her head and muttered, "That's not the same."

After a moment Bridget said, "You're quite right, my
dear. Of course, it's not the same. A gypsy life is all very

well for adults who choose it, but children want security and permanence, the way Damon, over there, wants his chair to be in the same spot by the fire every night. It was a foolish thing for me to say." She leaned forward and put her hand on Robin's. "But people *do* have to count on other people, Robin, no matter how frightening and dangerous that seems at times. If you give up on people, you're giving up on life."

Robin stood up stiffly and pulled her lips into a smile. "I understand," she said. "I understand, but I have to go now. It's dark, and my folks will be worried."

Bridget started to get up. "Wait," she said. "I'll go part of the way with you. You shouldn't be out alone so late at night."

"Oh, no," Robin said quickly. "I'm not afraid. If I run, I can be there in a minute."

Outside the gate she turned and looked back. She watched the slice of light narrow and disappear as Bridget closed the cottage door. Then she turned away, but not toward the orchard and the Village. As fast as she could, in the misty darkness, Robin made her way toward Palmeras House and the Velvet Room.

Terror in the Dark

When Robin reached the grove of trees, she had to slow to a walk and feel her way with outstretched hands. The air was so thick and damp it was like walking through rain clouds that had fallen to the ground. She couldn't even see Palmeras House until she reached the patio, and even then it was only a great blurry mass of deeper darkness against a dark sky.

Like a blind person, she found her way to the well. Her feet told her the way over the bricks of the patio floor, and her fingers remembered how to turn the key in the padlock. Then, at the bottom of the ladder, her groping hands found the candle and matches, and at last her eyes were useful again.

Inside the empty rooms of Palmeras House it was even darker than it had been the night before. But, as Robin tiptoed through the house, shielding the flame of her candle with her cupped hand, a fear hovered somewhere in the back of her mind that had nothing to do with the dark shadows that filled the corners. Just as the candle's light held back the shadows, a part of her mind was holding back the fear—keeping it nameless and shapeless until she reached the Velvet Room.

She got to the top of the stairs and glided down the long hall to the door. She opened it with a feeling of triumph. She'd made it! But this time it didn't work.

Instead of fading, the fear grew and took shape. Something had happened to the magic of the Velvet Room. It was not the same. It didn't look any different. It was all there just as it had always been. As she moved forward, the candle's light fell on the same familiar things: the tiny inlaid game table, the chair with roses on it, the curving back of the velvet couch. But somehow there was a difference.

Feeling dazed and desolate, she drifted into the alcove and sat down. In the velvet circle, if anywhere at all, she might be able to recapture the missing magic. But nothing happened, and she found herself thinking instead of Bridget's story. As she went over in her mind all the things that Bridget had told her, she began to feel again the excitement she had felt in the cottage. And then, without realizing it, she was thinking about what Bridget meant when she asked if Robin understood. Reluctantly at first, and then more eagerly, she began to explore some ideas that she had been carefully avoiding.

Before Robin noticed that her candle was burning low, she had discovered some pretty amazing things. She had discovered, she thought, what Bridget had meant when she had talked about good and bad reasons and the importance of counting on people. And she had also found out what it was that was different about the Velvet Room. Tonight, for the first time, she understood what the Velvet Room really was, and maybe even more important, what it wasn't and never could be. What it really was, was just what you could see by the candle's light—a beautiful room full of lovely old things. And what it wasn't, was what Robin had tried to make it—an enchanted refuge, a strictly private world of dreams.

As she moved slowly toward the door, Robin stopped to look at everything and say good-by. She knew she would never forget even the tiniest thing. But she also knew, now that leaving it would only be the end of an adventure; not the end of everything. And it *had* been a wonderful adventure—meeting Bridget, exploring the tunnel, finding the Velvet Room. There must be hundreds of people who grew up and grew old without ever having—

Suddenly Robin froze into rigid attention. Into the midst of her musing had come a strange sound. For a moment she couldn't tell what it was or from what direction it came. As it grew louder and nearer, it became recognizable as the sound of tires on gravel, and she hurried back to look out the window. Below, on the gravel driveway, a car was approaching. It was going very slowly, and it had no headlights on. Like a giant night beetle, it crept up the road and stopped at the foot of the stairs that led to the main entrance of Palmeras House.

Robin could barely see the three shadowy figures that got out of the car, but she clearly heard the thuds as the car doors shut behind them. She pressed her nose against the window and peered downward. Just as the figures disappeared beneath the portico, a light flashed on. Someone had turned on a flashlight.

"Robbers!" she thought in terror. There could be no other reason for anyone to arrive at a deserted house at night in a car with headlights out. But then her panic subsided. Surely they wouldn't be able to get in. There was the big extra padlock on the front door, and all the other doors and windows were boarded up as well as locked.

She jumped off the window seat and tiptoed across the room to the door. She opened it and leaned out into the hall, listening. Almost immediately she heard the squeak of the hinges of the heavy double doors of the main entry. Somehow the robbers had gotten inside the house, and they had done it as quickly as if the front door had not been locked at all.

In blind panic Robin dashed back to the alcove. The candle went out in the rush of wind, but her groping hands found the heavy drapes and she slipped behind them. Fear was a great knot filling her throat and almost strangling her as she pressed herself back against the wall and listened to the footsteps on the stairway leading to the second floor.

The footsteps got nearer and louder, and then the door to the Velvet Room opened. Through the drapery Robin could see a faint glow of light. A voice said, "Here it is. Over this way."

Robin stifled a gasp of surprise. The voice was familiar. For a moment she couldn't think to whom it belonged, but as the footsteps came toward her, muffled now by the thick rug, she suddenly remembered. It was Fred Criley!

The footsteps stopped. From somewhere on the window side of the room a voice said, "That them?"

"Yeah." It was Fred again.

A third voice asked, "You got the key to this thing?"

"No," Fred said. "Old man McCurdy hangs on to that."

"Well, that ain't hard to fix."

There was a crash and then the tinkle of shattered

glass. For a moment Robin was almost more indignant than frightened. Someone must have broken the beautiful curved glass of the whatnot case.

"Yeah!" one of the strange voices said. "Pretty nice. I know a place in L.A. where these things will bring a handful of dough."

For a minute the only sound was the scrape and tinkle of objects being taken from the glass case and dropped into something, perhaps a bag. Then one of the strange voices said, "That just about does it. Come on, let's get out of here."

"Wait a minute," Fred's voice said. "I got something else to do first. If these things just turn up missing, it ain't going to look too good for my family. Outside of old man McCurdy, my ma's the only one who ever has the keys to this place. So I'm gonna fix it so no one's ever gonna know there's been any robbery."

"Oh, yeah? How're you gonna do that?"

"It's a cinch. We set fire to the place; it burns down, and nobody's ever gonna know whether them little things is in all those ashes or not."

Robin's heart stood still with dismay. No one spoke for a moment, and then one of the strangers said, "Well, suit yourself, but I ain't gonna help. This place gives me the creeps. I'll wait in the car."

"Me, too," the other voice said. "Ya know, when we first got out of the car down there, I thought I saw a little light in one of the windows up here. I heard tell, lots of times, that this place is haunted. You burn 'er down if you want to, but I'm getting out of here right now."

Robin heard Fred's short hard laugh. "What a couple of chicken livers. O.K. Go hide in the car. I'll be down in a minute."

Footsteps crossed the room. "Wait a minute," Fred called. "How'm I gonna see if you take the flashlight?"

"That's your problem. We gotta get down these stairs, don't we? You start that there fire, and you'll have lots of light."

The footsteps went out the door and down the hall. There was the sound of a match striking and the smell of sulfur. Robin could hear Fred moving around on the other side of the room. With only a match's flame on the other side of the room, the alcove was left in complete darkness, so it seemed safe to peek around the edge of the drape. Fred was over by the bookshelves. With one hand, he was holding a lighted match and with the other, he was pulling books off the shelf and dropping them on the floor. Then he crouched down and shoved the books into a pile. The match burned low and he dropped it. There was a scratching sound, and another match flared up. Robin watched in horror as Fred leaned over and held the flame to the pages of an open book.

Without even knowing that she was going to do it, Robin leaped out from behind the drape and screamed "STOP!" with every ounce of power in her lungs. Fred catapulted into the air and whirled to face the darkness in the alcove, his eyes bulging wildly in his pudgy face. Staggering backward, he tripped over a footstool, and his howl of fear was cut short with a heavy thud as he landed on his back.

If she had stayed in the alcove, Fred might have gotten up and run away without ever knowing what had screamed at him out of the darkness. But the book was burning brightly, and Robin couldn't bear it. She dashed into the room, and, grabbing the book by the cover, she began to beat it on the floor.

In a moment the fire was out, and the room was once again in darkness, but before the light had died away Fred Criley recognized Robin. Just as she dropped the book and began to back away, he spoke again, not frightened now, but hard and angry. "What are you doin' here?" Robin heard him move closer in the darkness. "Come here!" He was so near that, as Robin turned to run, she felt the rush of air as his hands swept past her.

He probably would have caught her before she even reached the door if she hadn't been so familiar with her surroundings. When she reached the door, Fred was still stumbling over furniture and swearing somewhere in the darkness behind her. For a terrible minute she couldn't find the doorknob, but then her fingers grasped it and she was out the door and on her way down the hall.

She was part way down the staircase to the first floor, feeling her way on the dark stairs with desperate haste, when there was a shout from behind her. "Hank! Jess! Stop her! Head her off!"

Robin stumbled at the bottom of the stairs, picked herself up, and dashed toward the front door. One of the big double doors was open; but just as she almost reached it, a figure appeared in the doorway, and she was caught in a blinding glare of light. Before she could stop, Robin almost collided with the man who held the light. With a startled yelp, the stranger raised the flashlight as if he meant to hit her with it, and in terror Robin threw up her hand to protect her head. Her upflung hand crashed against the flashlight with painful force, and there was a spinning arc of light as it flew from his hand. Darkness and silence followed the crash of the flashlight to the stone floor of the portico.

Realizing that she must be almost close enough to

the stranger to touch him, Robin began to back away as silently as she could. She had gone only a few steps when the stranger shouted, "Hey, Fred! What's going on? Who's in there?"

Fred's voice was close now, too. He must be almost down the stairs. "It's a little kid from the Village. We got to catch her. Where's Hank?"

"Right here." The other one had apparently reached the door.

Only a few feet away Robin continued to edge backward, step by step. She knew that the door to the drawing room was very close. Her fingers touched the wall, and she turned and felt frantically for the door and the doorknob.

"Shhh! Listen, I heard something. Over that way." Shuffling feet were feeling their way toward her when at last she found the doorknob. The click when it turned brought shouts from her three pursuers, and they lunged toward her. Robin slipped through the door and ran. If she could only find her way to the adobe wing and the secret door behind the bookcase before they caught her!

She had the advantage of knowing her way around in the big house, and she might have eluded them entirely in the darkness except for the old doors. Each time her shuffling, groping pursuers fell a little behind, there was another door to go through; and the squeak of the stiff old hinges brought them after her again in stumbling haste. Then the door into the adobe wing stuck and she had to jerk it several times before it would open. By that time the footsteps were very close. "Here she is," a voice shouted. "I got her!" But the door came open, and Robin ducked down and slipped through. The three followed very close behind.

"I saw her," someone yelled. "She went over that way."

"Good," it was Fred's voice this time. "There's no door on that side of the room. We've got her trapped. Spread out and close in on her."

Sobs of fear tore at Robin's throat as she felt frantically for the catch to the secret door. She found it, swung the bookcase out, slipped behind it and closed it, just as someone reached the other side. As she leaned against the back of the bookcase and fought to quiet her sobs, she could hear the brushing sound of groping hands on the front of the shelves.

"I got her! I got her!" someone yelled.

"Turn loose, you fool, it's me."

There were more bumping, stumbling noises, and then Fred said, "You must've have let her slip between you. I know she was here. I heard her bawling."

"Well she's not here now. I don't know who let her get past, but she's gone."

"She can't get far. Not if we don't let her get back to the front door. There ain't no other way out of this place. Jess, you go back and guard the front door. Hank, go back the way we come. I'll go this way. She has to be here some'eres." The shuffling footsteps began again and slowly faded away.

When all was quiet on the other side of the bookcase, Robin felt her way to the stone steps that led down to the tunnel. Part way down the stairs her breath began to come in quick hard gasps and her legs shook so violently that she could hardly control them. Now that she had eluded her pursuers and was no longer running, perhaps for her life, a reaction set in. Several times she had to stop and lean against the wall. She couldn't seem to get enough air, and the top of her head felt as if it had come loose and was about to float away. After a while, without quite knowing how, she found herself climbing the ladder that led out of the well. The next thing she remembered was being in the orchard, stumbling on the furrowed ground, and hanging on to the branches of the orange trees to keep from falling. There were glimpses of other things: the eucalyptus trees, the barnyard, the gravel road under her feet. Somewhere along the way she realized her hand was hurting and tears were pouring down her face. Finally, there was the smoothness of mowed grass under her feet, and then she was pounding on the back door of the McCurdys' house.

Lights came on in the house, and the door was opened by Mr. McCurdy, with Carmela peeking out from behind him.

"Mr. McCurdy," Robin gasped, "Palmeras House. They're trying to burn it down. You've got to stop them!"

Dreams—Lost and Found

WHEN ROBIN woke up, she was lying in a big soft bed in a strange room. It was a bright sunny day, but there was a late feeling, as if she had been asleep for a long time. There was a dull throbbing in her hand. She pulled it out from under the covers and saw that it was wrapped in a heavy bandage. She wondered vaguely what had happened to it.

"Robin." It was Mama's voice. "How do you feel, honey?"

Robin turned her head. Mama was sitting in a chair on the other side of the bed. She looked different at first, tired and sad, until her same old smile brightened the faded prettiness of her face. Robin smiled back. "I feel fine," she said. "My hand just hurts a little."

Mama came around and sat on the edge of the bed and took Robin's unbandaged hand in hers. Suddenly Robin remembered. All at once everything that had happened came back. "Mama," she asked, "did they burn it down? Did Palmeras House burn down?"

"No, honey," Mama said. "Nothing burned down at all."

"But what happened?" Robin begged. "Did Mr. Mc-Curdy get there in time to stop them?"

"I don't know just what did happen. I've been in here with you most of the time, and I haven't had a chance to hear what's been happening. But your dad did tell me that nothing burned down. Don't worry about it." Mama got up. "I'm just going to run downstairs and tell everybody that you're awake and feeling better. They're all worried about you."

By now Robin had recognized the room as one of the guest rooms in the McCurdy house, but she still couldn't remember how she had gotten there. In fact, she couldn't remember anything at all from the time she reached the McCurdy house. There had been Mr. McCurdy's startled face and her own voice screaming, "You've got to stop them! You've got to stop them!" After that there was a faint memory of being carried somewhere and of her hand hurting and hurting, and that was all.

It seemed strange to be lying in bed in the middle of the day when she didn't feel a bit sick. Robin threw back the covers and sat up. She was wearing a soft night-gown with a tucked yoke and ruffles. One of Gwen's, she decided. When she tried standing up, there was a weak feeling somewhere in her middle, but it felt mostly like hunger.

The door flew open, and Gwen dashed in, a whirlwind of dimples and bouncing blond curls. "Hi!" she said, and just stood there glowing.

"Hi," Robin grinned back.

"Gee, I thought you'd never wake up. I've been dying

to talk to you. How'd you stop them from burning down the house? What happened to your hand? And what did you do— Hey," she broke off, "do you feel all right?"

"I'm just a little dizzy," Robin said. "I guess it's because I'm hungry. What time is it, anyway? I feel as if I haven't eaten for a year."

"No wonder," Gwen said. "It's almost four o'clock. Let's go down and get Carmela to fix you something. Here, lean on my shoulder."

"O.K.," Robin said. "I don't know what made me sleep so long. I always wake up early, no matter what."

"You had a sleeping pill," Gwen said. "Don't you remember? When you first got here last night, you were crying and fainting and everything; so, when Doctor Woods got here, he said you were hysterical, and he gave you a pill." They started down the stairs with Robin's arm around Gwen's shoulders. "Boy!" Gwen went on, "I sure wish I'd been awake. For once, something exciting happens around here, and I don't know anything about it till it's all over."

When they were almost to the bottom, they met Mama and Dad and the McCurdys coming up. Everybody started talking at once, and Robin couldn't hear what anyone was saying. Pretty soon, though, everyone was telling everyone else that they mustn't ask Robin any questions until she'd had a chance to eat something.

In the dining room the big table was set for just one person. Mr. McCurdy pulled back the chair for Robin, and Carmela came in with a tray. After Robin sat down, everyone else sat around the table, watching her as if she were singing a song or saying a poem, instead of just eating some bacon and eggs. When she was almost finished, Mr. McCurdy said, "There's a police officer waiting to talk to you, Robin, as soon as you feel able."

Robin gulped and almost choked on a mouthful of toast. "I'll talk to him now," she said. "I feel O.K.—I think." Suddenly, what she was really feeling was—scared. With the mention of the policeman, it occurred to her for the first time that she was going to have to explain her own presence in Palmeras House last night. And how *could* she do that? How could she even explain how she'd gotten in without giving away Bridget's secret?

She was just wondering if anyone would believe that she had walked in the front door after the robbers had gone in, when Mr. McCurdy took something out of his pocket and laid it on the table. It was the key to the tunnel! Robin's hand flew to her throat. Sure enough, the key was gone. Mr. McCurdy smiled. "Yes, that's where we found it," he said. "Before I call Officer Talbot in, I certainly would like to know where you found it, Robin. I have one just like it, but I never even knew there was a duplicate until last night when Doctor Woods found this hanging around your neck."

Possible explanations, none of them very believable, flopped around in Robin's mind. She couldn't tell Bridget's secret, but she had never been very good at telling a lie. Even Shirley always knew when she was fooling. But she had to try. As she started to stammer something, Mr. Mc-Curdy's question came back into her mind. "Found it?" she said. "Oh yes . . . I found it . . . in this old box . . . er . . . way down in the bottom . . . under some things." To her amazement, everyone seemed to be listening respectfully, as if she were making sense. She hurried on before anyone could ask where the box had been. "And then I found out that it opened the well, sort of by accident. I was sitting on the well lid one day, and I just happened to notice the padlock. So I tried the key, and it worked, and then I started just going into the house sometimes, through the tunnel . . ."

Mama gasped and shook her head reprovingly.

"Oh, I never hurt anything or took anything," Robin said. "I just went in there sometimes. I've been doing it ever since last summer, and I've never hurt anything. But last night . . ."

At that point Mr. McCurdy got up. "Wait a minute, Robin," he said. "I think Officer Talbot would like to hear the rest of your story."

Robin put her hand on his sleeve. "Mr. McCurdy," she said quickly. "Did you get the things back? The pictures and things that belong in the glass case?"

"No, not yet. Just as I got there last night, I got a glimpse of the car. It was leaving the gate, and I caught it in my headlights for a split second. I was able to get part of the license number, and the police are working on that; but so far they've had no luck. It would help if you were able to describe the men."

Robin thought a moment. "No, not two of them. I heard their voices, but I didn't get a good look at them. But I could describe Fred Criley."

"Fred Criley!" Mr. McCurdy banged his fist down on the table. "I knew it had to be someone who'd had a chance to have those keys copied." He hurried out and returned with a policeman. "Robin," he said, "this is Officer Talbot. He'd like to ask you a few questions."

The policeman wanted to know how many men there were and what they looked like and what the car looked like. Some of the questions Robin could answer, and some she couldn't. Then the policeman said, "There'll probably be some more things we'll have to know later, but I'm going to get this out right away. It ought to help a lot. Thank you, Miss; you've been a big help."

When the officer had gone, Mrs. McCurdy said, "Now suppose we all keep quiet and let Robin tell what happened in her own words. Right from the beginning."

So Robin started at the beginning: when she had decided to stop at Palmeras House for a short visit on her way home from Bridget's. She told about the robbers coming right into the room while she was hiding behind the drapes in the alcove, about nearly colliding with one of the men in the doorway of Palmeras House, and about knocking the flashlight down. At that point she suddenly realized what had happened to her hand.

"That's it," she said. "That's how my hand got hurt. I thought he was going to hit me with the flashlight, and I threw my hand up. I remember its hurting when the flashlight hit it, but then I don't remember even feeling it again until I was almost to the McCurdys' house."

When Robin had told everything she could remember, Mr. McCurdy told what had happened after Robin had given the alarm. "Catherine and Carmela took Robin up to bed and called Doctor Woods, and I jumped into the car and headed for Palmeras House. Just as I got to the gate, I saw an old car roar out of the drive and down the highway. I managed to get the first three numbers of the license, but I didn't try to follow, because at that point I was more interested in trying to save what I could in the old place, if it really was on fire. When I got to the house, there wasn't any fire, but in the library I found that someone had tried to start one with a pile of books. And I also found that the whatnot case had been broken into and robbed. I was puzzled by the fact that the locks on the front door and the padlock on the gate had all been opened and showed no sign of damage, as if the thieves had had the keys. But I knew that the only keys were in the safe here at home."

Just then Gwen broke in excitedly. "Fred had the keys last Saturday when his mother was cleaning in the house. Remember, Robin, Fred unlocked the doors for his mother and Carmela? And remember how interested he was in the portraits because there were jewels in the frames?"

"He must have kept the keys while his mother and Carmela cleaned," Mr. McCurdy said. "They were there most of the day, so there was plenty of time for him to take the keys to town and get copies made."

"I guess he didn't try again to start a fire," Robin said.

"Well, there wasn't much point in a fire to cover up the robbery after you'd gotten away to tell on them. My guess is that when they finally realized you'd escaped, they got panicky. They didn't even bother to close the doors behind them." Mr. McCurdy shook his head ruefully. "If those stupid kids had only known—some of the old books they were planning to burn up are worth a good deal more than the things they took. And, of course, the historical value of the things in Palmeras House and of the house itself, for that matter, is immeasurable."

"Perhaps you know, Robin," Mrs. McCurdy said, "that my husband's fondest dream has been to make Palmeras House into a county museum. So, you see, you saved a dream last night."

Robin felt her face getting hot, so she looked down and away. "Well, I guess things were just meant to happen the way they did," Dad said. "I was just thinking that the weather deserves some credit, too. Those boys might have staged their robbery several nights ago if it hadn't been for the cold spell. They wouldn't have dared to risk running into the smudging crews."

"That's right," Mr. McCurdy said. "They had to wait for a warm night. I hadn't thought of that." After a moment he laughed. "I'll bet it's not often that a citrus rancher has a reason to be thankful for a spell of freezing weather. But most of all, we're grateful to Robin."

"We certainly are," Mrs. McCurdy said. "But right now I'm afraid that Robin ought to be getting back upstairs. Doctor Woods said that she was to spend the day in bed."

Dad walked back to the room with Robin and tucked her in. "When did you and Mama get here?" she asked him. "Did the McCurdys tell you I was here?"

"Well, last night, when it began to get late and you hadn't come back from Bridget's, I walked over there to get you. But when I got to the cottage, Bridget said you'd been gone for over an hour. That really scared me, but I thought you might possibly have come over here to see Gwen. So I came on over. I guess I got here right after you did, because Doctor Woods was just bandaging your hand. I tried to talk to you, but you'd had a pill and were pretty groggy. After you went to sleep, I went back home for a while, and this morning Mama and I came back."

"Bridget!" Robin said. "She must be worried. Has anyone gone over to tell her that I'm all right?"

"Yes, Bridget knows. As soon as I got home last night, I sent Rudy over to tell her that we'd found you and you were all right." Dad sat down in the chair by the bed. "By the way, Robin," he said. "I can understand about the old house—why you kept it a secret and all. I'd have been crazy about a secret like that when I was your age."

"Have you been there?" Robin asked in surprise.

"Just this morning," Dad said. "While you were still

asleep, Mr. McCurdy took me over and showed me all around. We had quite a conversation. It's been a long time since I've done much reading about California history, but a bit of it came back. There are a lot of books in that library that I'd like to read. Wonderful stuff. First editions and early records." There was a look in Dad's eyes that Robin remembered from a long time in the past.

Robin was sure that with all the sleep she'd already had there wasn't much use trying to go to sleep again. But the sedative must not have worn off entirely because she began to feel very vague and dreamy. Her thoughts started drifting up and down like waves. Up—into an idea, and down—into soft comfortable fuzziness. "I saved Palmeras House . . ." she thought. "I saved the Velvet Room . . . Now we're even . . . Mrs. McCurdy said I saved a dream. I guess I lost one, too, but that's all right. Dreams have to end when you wake up . . . I'm awake now . . ."

Dad was standing up slowly, trying to be quiet. "I'm awake now," Robin said out loud. Dad sat back down, and Robin groped sleepily for his hand. "I wanted to tell you something," she said, and her voice sounded slow and mumbly, even to herself. "I almost forgot. I wanted to tell you that I'm going, too. I'm going with you when you go to Uncle Joe's."

Good-bys Aren't Easy

IT HAD BEEN decided that Robin was to stay at the Mc-Curdys' until the following morning, when Doctor Woods would be back to look at her hand. She had a late supper in bed in the guest room next to Gwen's—the room that was to have been hers. Gwen brought a tray up, too, and ate with Robin to keep her company. Something, perhaps a letdown after all the excitement or the aftereffects of the sedative, made Robin feel silly and lightheaded. They got the giggles over something and laughed until absolutely everything seemed hysterically funny. They kept on laughing until their sides ached and tears rolled down their faces.

Once in a while Robin stopped laughing long enough to remember that she would have to tell Gwen about the decision not to stay. But she couldn't do it just then. It would have to be sometime when she could go home to the cabin right afterward.

The next morning Robin was trying to make the bed —the big soft bed, almost three times as wide as the one she shared with Theda—when there was a knock on the door. It wasn't Gwen, as she expected, but Mr. McCurdy. He asked how she was feeling and peeked under the bandages on her hand to see if the swelling had gone down any. Then, just as she thought he was leaving, he sat down instead and just looked at her.

"Robin," he said. "I've been puzzled about something, and maybe you could set me straight. It's about that key you found, the one to the underground exit."

Robin swallowed hard. She should have known it was too good to be true—everyone's accepting her story about finding the key. Her folks could, perhaps, because they didn't know much about Palmeras House, but not the McCurdys.

'You said you found it in a box," Mr. McCurdy was saying. "Could you tell me where the box was?"

"Well," Robin began, keeping her eyes down, "it was in this old wooden box . . . down in the . . . that is, it was in the . . ." Then she broke down altogether and said nothing at all for a moment. Finally she gave up with an anguished wail. "I can't tell you! I can't tell you! I promised!"

Mr. McCurdy took her hand and pulled her down on the footstool beside him. "Here now," he said. "Don't get yourself all upset. You don't have to tell me anything if you don't want to. And I wouldn't ask you to break any promises. But how would it be if I already knew the secret you're keeping. Then it wouldn't be breaking a promise to talk about it, would it?"

Robin shook her head slowly. "I guess not."

"Well then, it occurred to me that you might have gotten the key from Bridget. Am I right?"

Robin stared in consternation. "Do you really know the secret?" she asked. "Bridget's secret?"

He nodded.

"But how? I mean, Bridget said that nobody knew, except me."

"A lawyer told me. When Bridget first came back to Santa Luisa, she went to see a lawyer about claiming part of Las Palmeras."

"Yes," Robin said, "I know. She told me that."

"Well, Bill Weber, the lawyer, happened to be a friend of mine. He thought Bridget might be a fake, and he came to the house that night to talk to me about it. She hadn't asked him to keep it secret at that time so he didn't feel he was betraying a confidence. It was the next day that she sent him a message saying she had decided not to tell, at least not right away. But I was sure she was no fake from the moment I saw her."

"Does Mrs. McCurdy know? And Gwen, too?"

"Not Gwen, but Mrs. McCurdy knows. I told her immediately; and when Bridget applied for the housekeeper's job, we decided to hire her and wait and see what would happen."

"Were you angry?" Robin asked. "I mean about her being Bonita?"

"Angry? No, I don't think we were angry. We were a little worried at first about what would happen, but you can't know Bridget for long and distrust her motives. As we got to know her better, we decided to respect her wish for secrecy and wait until she was ready to tell us. And she never has. How did she happen to tell you?"

Robin took a deep breath and told Mr. McCurdy all about it: that she hadn't known Bridget's secret until Friday evening, when Bridget had told her to keep her from making a big mistake. She tried to explain, without hurting Mr. McCurdy's feelings, that even though she liked him and Gwen and Mrs. McCurdy, she had really been going to stay because of the Velvet Room. "I guess it sounds crazy," she said. "But I'd started believing it was more important than anything else. And Bridget wanted me to see that it shouldn't make that much difference."

Mr. McCurdy nodded in a way that made Robin know he understood. "We'll be sorry to see you go," he said. "But I think you've made an admirable decision. To tell you the truth, Robin, I wasn't happy about taking you away from your family. They're a fine bunch, and you're important to them."

Mr. McCurdy was starting out the door when Robin called him back. "I was just thinking about what you said about Bridget," she said. "That you weren't angry that she was really Bonita."

"Yes?" Mr. McCurdy nodded.

"Well, when I asked Bridget why she hadn't told anybody who she was, she said it was mostly because she liked you and Mrs. McCurdy so much. She didn't want to risk changing you, the way her aunt and uncle were changed when they found out that Las Palmeras was going to belong to her. I was just thinking it might make her happy to know that you know and you're not angry about it."

Mr. McCurdy didn't say anything for a while, but then he put his hand on Robin's shoulder and said, "You may be right. We'll have to think about it."

The next Tuesday morning Robin woke up reluctantly. It was the Williamses' last day at Las Palmeras. Dad had already postponed their departure for two days, and there was no reason to do it again. Uncle Joe was probably going to be mad as it was.

Not that they could have helped it, because they

couldn't. The police had wanted Robin handy in case there were more questions, and Doctor Woods had wanted to be sure there were no bones broken in her hand. But yesterday Fred Criley had come back and turned himself in, and his two accomplices had been captured in Los Angeles; so the police didn't need Robin any longer. And the swelling was almost gone from her hand.

So Wednesday the bags and boxes would be back on the roof and running boards of the Model T, and the Williams family would be back on the road again. The thought made Robin close her eyes tight and hope she really wasn't awake. But, of course, she was.

When she opened her eyes and thought about it clearly, she realized this wasn't quite as bad as all the other times. At least there was an end in sight. It was much better to be going somewhere instead of anywhere—even if it was only to Uncle Joe's.

Uncle Joe's! What would it be like to live there? It didn't seem probable that Uncle Joe would have changed for the better, but maybe he wasn't as bad as Robin remembered him. It was hard to picture the tourist cottages exactly, but it seemed as if some of them were almost as big as the cabins in Palmeras Village. Besides, the cottages had indoor bathrooms, which was certainly an improvement. And if they were fixed up a bit, they might not be so desolate looking. Uncle Joe had said in his letter that he was going to open them for tourists again—so maybe he would have some painting done. Perhaps he'd even plant a little lawn.

The sound of someone moving across the room interrupted Robin's thoughts. It was Rudy getting up to light the fire in the stove. In a few minutes he crawled back into his cot to wait for the room to warm up. Cary

was still sound asleep at the other end of the bed, curled up in a small mound. Near him, on the floor, were his sword and shield, and his hand on the pillow was clenched into a fist.

"Poor Cary," Robin thought suddenly, and then wondered why. It had something to do with the clenched fist and the beat-up old garbage-can lid. It wasn't much of a shield for somebody so little and so determined about everything. Thinking about Cary, Robin smiled suddenly. He'd been so funny the last few days. He'd been telling everyone that Robin had saved Palmeras House. In Cary's version, one of the bandits hit Robin's hand with a great big flashlight, but she just took it away from him and hit him right back. And then she put out a huge fire and chased the bandits away all by herself. And, as Cary put it, Robin was a "hero" and would probably get a golden medal. It had gotten so that every time Robin went outside, all the younger Village kids gathered around her and reverently asked to see her bandaged hand. She tried to explain that Cary had exaggerated just a bit, but she couldn't help feeling pleased by all that admiration and awe.

She sighed and tucked her feet up against Theda's warm back. She would have missed Cary if she'd decided to stay with Gwen. Cary—and Shirley, too, funny little frightened Shirley, and—everybody. She was glad, really *glad*, they wouldn't be driving away tomorrow without her. That was one thing she was sure of, even if she couldn't be glad about leaving Las Palmeras.

It hadn't been easy giving it all up. There had been times when she had wavered. One of the worst had been when she had to tell Gwen. Gwen had cried and cried, and Robin had felt just awful. She hadn't believed before that it mattered that much to Gwen. Down underneath she had thought that it was a sort of whim of Gwen's— like wanting to have a party or a certain kind of new coat. But Gwen didn't cry about things like coats and parties.

There had been another bad time when she had had to go to Lincoln School for her transfer. She had counted so much on finishing the year at Lincoln—one whole year at the same school.

But perhaps hardest of all had been saying good-by to Bridget. But at least she didn't have to worry about Bridget's being lonely and unhappy. The McCurdys had told her that they knew her secret. Bridget was happier than she'd been in years. Not that it meant much of a change in her life—she was quite content in her little cottage with her animal family—but it was nice, she said, to feel she was a McCurdy again. And Mr. McCurdy had asked her to help him with a history of Las Palmeras. She was really excited about that. He'd even asked her to serve as an advisor on the board of his historical society.

The cabin was warmer now, so Robin slid out of bed and got down the coffee pot. She filled it with water from the old green faucet and put it on the stove. It was going to be a busy day for all the Williamses. They might as well get started.

Want to Come Along?

ROBIN WAS ALONE in the cabin that afternoon when she heard a car pull up and stop out in front. Mama, Theda, and Shirley had gone to the Bryants', three cabins down the row. Mama was returning some borrowed sugar, and Theda went along because of Joy Bryant. Joy was about Theda's age, and they had a lot in common—like boys and favorite movie stars. Dad and Rudy were out back working on the Model T; and where Cary was, was anybody's guess, as usual.

So Robin was alone. She had been sitting on the cot folding and packing dresses, but when she heard the car, she looked out the window. It was the McCurdys' big maroon Buick. Mr. McCurdy got out and came up the stairs. He was dressed in a dark business suit and tie instead of the stock pants and wool shirt he usually wore. Robin ran to the door.

"Hi," she said. "Won't you come in?"

"Hello, Robin. How's that hand feeling today?"

"Oh, it's fine. It doesn't hurt at all anymore."

"Well, that's good news." Mr. McCurdy stepped into the cabin and looked around. "Aren't your folks at home?"

"Dad's out back. I'll call him." Robin pulled a chair away from the table and took a half-packed cardboard box off it. "Won't you sit down?"

In back of the cabin, Dad and Rudy were only partly visible. Dad's head was out of sight under the Model T's hood, and only Rudy's legs protruded from under the front bumper. Dad pulled his head out at Robin's call and came up the back stairs, wiping his hands on an oily rag.

"Dad," Robin said. "Mr. McCurdy is here to see you."

Mr. McCurdy stood up and held out his hand as Dad came in. "Hello, Paul," he said. "I see I caught you in the midst of something."

Dad grinned. "Nothing that won't wait. We're just trying to stick the old car together so it'll stay in one piece as far as Fresno. Sit down, Mr. McCurdy. Robin, how about a couple of cups of coffee?"

As Robin poured coffee into the two best mugs, she felt a strange uncertain excitement begin to teeter up her spine. She had a feeling— But just then Mr. McCurdy said, "You run on into the other room, Robin. What I have to say to your dad had better be confidential for the time being."

So, for an endless time, Robin sat on the bed and wondered, while voices too soft to hear rose and fell in the other room. But at last Dad's voice called, "Robin!" and she catapulted out the door. One look at Dad's face told her that whatever Mr. McCurdy had said had been something good—very good.

"Well, Robin," Dad said, as she groped her way into a chair, "it looks like the Williams family won't be leaving

Las Palmeras tomorrow after all."

"I'll be glad to hear what Robin thinks about this arrangement," Mr. McCurdy said. "After all, if it hadn't been for her, there'd be quite a different situation for all of us." He turned to Robin. "You remember hearing about the historical society that has been planning to make Palmeras House into a museum of county history? Well, the members have put off doing anything about it for almost five years now. Of course, there has been good reason. All the members are busy people, and money isn't too plentiful these days. But it occurred to me that this might be a good time to prod them a bit—with the paper full of the close call the old place had last Friday. So I called an emergency board meeting for this morning." He smiled and pointed to the suit he was wearing. "In fact, I'm on my way home from the meeting right now. And just as I'd hoped, the board decided to get our plans for Palmeras House moving immediately, in a small way at first . . ."

"Then you're going to fix it all up again?" Robin asked. "I mean, take the boards off the windows and make the lawn grow and everything?"

"Why, yes," Mr. McCurdy said.

"Oh," Robin breathed, "that's wonderful."

Mr. McCurdy looked at her curiously. "Well, yes," he said. "But I haven't even gotten to the part I thought you'd like. On my recommendation," he went on, "the board offered your father the job of custodian and watchman for the new museum, and he has just accepted."

Robin jumped to her feet and started to throw her arms around her father's neck, but she stopped almost in mid-air. "Will it be good for you?" she asked. "I mean, will it be not too much exertion, like the doctor said? Will it be as good as keeping the store for Uncle Joe?"

Dad only nodded, but Mr. McCurdy said, "I think it will be just right for your father. I plan to have some of the orchard men take care of the grounds, so there'll be very little physical labor. Mostly just dusting and sweeping and keeping an eye on things. And with your father's background, I wouldn't be surprised if he eventually became a curator and guide." He grinned at Robin. "There's a part of the job that I think might be turned over to you, at least on weekends. There'll be a desk in the entry hall with a registration book for guests, postcards, information —that sort of thing. Think you could help out there?"

"Oh, yes," Robin said. "Oh, yes, I'd like that. And I could help with other things, too. I could help take care of everything, couldn't I?"

"I don't see why not," Mr. McCurdy said, laughing. "I'd say you had a pretty good start in that department. Well, I've got to be on my way, or Catherine will think something has happened to me. I'm glad things worked out this way. Very glad. And wait till I tell Gwen. You'd better come over soon, Robin, and help her celebrate."

As Robin stood on the front steps waving good-by to Mr. McCurdy, it was all she could do to keep from bouncing up and down the way Shirley always did when she was happy. When the Buick disappeared through the eucalyptus hedge, she ran back and hugged Dad until she almost choked him. Then she grabbed the box she'd been packing and dumped it out on the bed. "I'm going to start unpacking," she said. "Won't Mama be surprised?"

"Wait just a minute," Dad said. "Hold on there. We *are* going to be moving—just not very far."

"Moving? Why? Where?"

"We can't stay here because the new man for the mule barns will need this house."

"But where are we going?" Robin asked.

Dad looked a little worried. "Mr. McCurdy said that in a few years they may be able to convert the old garage out behind Palmeras House into a nice little home. But in the meantime, we're to have the back rooms in the east wing of the old house. You know, they're set off by themselves on the other side of the dining hall. We'll have the kitchen, the breakfast room, and four little rooms that used to be servants' quarters. Mr. McCurdy wants me right there where I can keep my eye on things at night as well as in the daytime." Dad put his hand on Robin's shoulder. "I know how much you've wanted us to have a home of our own. This won't be quite the same. But Mama will love that huge kitchen with all those cupboards, and we'll have lots more space than we do here."

Robin laughed right out loud. For once Dad didn't seem to know how she felt about something. "Oh, Dad," she said. "It's wonderful. I don't care if it's not a house just like everybody else's. And it doesn't matter that it's not really ours, either. What matters is . . ." She stopped for a moment, trying to decide just what it was that did matter so much. "I guess it's mostly having the same place long enough to feel that we belong somewhere. And . . . well, it ought to be beautiful and look as if it was really meant for people."

Dad laughed. "And how do you decide if a house was really meant for people?"

"Well, for one thing, it ought to look as if it would last for ages. It takes such a long time for people to grow up and get old. It seems to me that houses ought to look strong and solid."

There was the sound of voices, and Mama, Theda, and Shirley came in the front door. Dad called Rudy out from under the car, and even Cary appeared from somewhere. For a long time cabin three of Palmeras Village was a confusion of questions and answers. And nobody seemed happier than Mama. No one had heard her mention it before, but it was suddenly clear that Mama had hated the thought of living at Uncle Joe's worse than—well, maybe even worse than Robin.

In the midst of all the excitement Robin slipped out the door and down the steps. She was almost to the orchard when there was a sound of footsteps right behind her.

"Hi," Cary said. "Are you 'wandering off' again?"

"No," Robin said quickly, and then to her surprise she realized it was true. It wasn't "wandering off" at all. There was none of the old feeling of things not being real—none of the confusion and need to get away. She just wanted to walk over to Palmeras House to look at it and think about how wonderful it was going to be to live there and help take care of it.

"No," she said again, "not really. I'm just going over to look around." She looked down at Cary's freckled face and bright blue eyes. "Want to come along?"

"Sure," Cary said.

In a few minutes they had climbed over the stone wall and were walking across the dead lawn. "See right up there?" Robin said. "That's the tower where I hid when the robbers came. It's part of a big library room that runs all along where those arched windows are. I'll show it to you once we get moved in."

She smiled at Cary who was gazing upward with round-eyed awe. "I used to call it the Velvet Room," she said.